SAVED BY THE SURLY MEDIC

HALEY TRAVIS

1

———

JONAH

The forest is perfect today.

Life just getting on with the business of growing. Everything is quiet, except for the tiny rustles of birds, squirrels, and the odd croak of a frog.

My boots trudge almost silently along Maple Trail. It's my turn to check the paths just before sunset to make sure nobody gets caught out in the woods after dark.

So far I've been pretty lucky, and the only mishaps on my watch have been teenagers with a twisted ankle, or couples who desperately realized they needed some bug spray at twilight. Ironic that I'm the one with the most medical training, yet I rarely come across anyone in the woods who really requires it.

As the sun begins to dip over the mountain peak, the long shadows become deeper, stretching out as they turn the greens to gray. The perfect stillness of the forest is broken when I reach the river. The light babble of the stream is a quiet companion as I continue walking.

The sound of the water grows louder as I near the rapids. The path takes a turn away from them, yet the water can still be heard bouncing across a half mile of jagged rock. There are several steep drops, which is why we've installed garish yellow signs beside the river at this point: "Rapids ahead — no boating past this point."

Personally, I wanted the sign to read, "Deadly rapids ahead. Choppy water and rocks will kill you. Don't be stupid." But I was outvoted.

I pause to watch the waves dance over a large rock right at the bend.

Then I hear a terrified squeal just up ahead.

My feet take me at top speed around the corner, where I see a young woman clutching the far side of the rock.

"Hold on," I bellow, making her flinch a bit in surprise. "I'm here to help."

She's facing the rock, but nods slightly, her voice drifting up faintly as she mutters something I can't make out.

She's shaking. I'm not surprised: at this time of year, the water is *cold*. I need to get her out of there before she loses all her strength.

I scan the edge of the river. This is the worst possible spot for me to try to get in. Thick spiky brush grows along one edge, and the only break in the scrub has some jagged rocks that might as well be knife blades.

Shit.

I have two choices: pull her up over the rock she's hanging onto and haul her out or tell her to let go and hope that she's able to grasp onto a couple of logs fifty feet downriver.

I carefully study the water patterns for a few seconds, then decide the current is too strong for the second option after yesterday's rain. Even if she's a good swimmer, there's maybe only a fifty-fifty shot of her getting close enough to the logs to grab on. They're probably slippery. And who knows what her grip strength is like.

Assessing the odds is part of what I do. She's already probably weakened from being so cold, and she's not exactly one of my former soldiers who signed up for danger.

It's option one. I'll have to pull her up over the rock.

Flinging my jacket to the ground, I wade into the river, then climb up over the rock. Reaching down, I grab her firmly by the forearm. She looks up at me...

And I'm instantly transported.

Her luminous light gray eyes are otherworldly. I'd say she's beautiful...except the word beautiful isn't strong or powerful enough. She's like a storybook goddess brought to life.

Inhaling sharply, I give my head a shake. I've been trained to ignore distractions. Focus, man.

"It's okay. I've got you. We have two choices," I tell her, forcing a smile to put her at ease and trying not to let my teeth chatter. "If I let you go, you'll have to twist, and then swim really hard and fast for those logs so that you don't go any further down river to the rapids."

I'm not going to mention that she could be torn apart by the ferocious rocks. She's trembling enough already.

"I'm not very strong," she mutters, teeth rattling.

"In that case, I'm just going to have to pull you up over this rock. Okay?"

"Okay. Thank you."

My teeth grit. "You need to keep your knees and feet engaged so that I'm not scraping all of your weight across your ribs. I don't want to hurt you more than I have to."

Her sweet smile sends a bizarre prickling sensation down my spine. "Rather...b-be dragged than tumble...hit r-rapids."

I spread my legs so I can grip the boulder with my thighs, stabilizing me as I grasp her other arm. Using my full strength, I pull her up, trying my best not to scrape her up too badly.

Suddenly her foot slips, and her entire weight comes down hard on the left side of her ribs. It takes more than a little scrambling, and grabbing her using a very inelegant hold, but eventually I manage to get her out of the river and on her feet in the shallow water.

The second the tension in her body releases, she begins to shiver from head to toe.

I hurry her onto the trail, then wrap my jacket around her narrow shoulders. "Thank you," she sputters. "Th-thought I was d-doomed."

We take a few steps, and she winces.

Pushing the jacket open, I look to check if her side is bleeding. Her eyes grow wide. "I'm a medic," I explain. "Does it feel like anything is broken?"

Her perfect, although still slightly bluish, lips turn up in the most incredible smile I've ever seen.

I've honestly never experienced a smile like this before. My guts might as well have been scrambled in those rapids. Swallowing hard, I try to focus on what she's saying.

"Not broken. Just...squished, I guess."

"May I do a quick check?"

"Sure." She lifts her left arm out of the way. I run my hand along the side of her ribs, right under her breast. Nothing feels out of place, thank goodness. "Can you take a full breath in for me, stretching out your lungs."

When she does so, she pulls a face. "Okay, that's uncomfortable, but I think everything's in working order."

"Good. You'd be cursing a blue streak, if anything was

cracked. Are you okay to walk to the trailhead, or do you want me to carry you?"

She tries to speak, then sputters, her teeth chattering from the cold, her head nodding furiously.

"I think your body just answered for you there." Scooping her up gently in my arms, she slings her right arm around my neck. I move slowly at first, waiting until she settles and gets comfortable. Then I pick up the pace, striding quickly toward my truck.

"I'm Brooke, by the way."

Typical. I'm holding a gorgeous woman in my arms, and I don't even think to introduce myself. What the hell is wrong with me? Dammit, this is why I'm single.

"Jonah. Jonah Wolfe."

Even though she's shivering, her smile is sassy. "You must be a bigshot. I've seen your name all over the place around here."

"Yeah, my family has roots in this mountain as deep as the trees'."

"I like the sound of that. It must feel incredible, belonging to a place."

Interesting. I never once thought of it like that.

It's impossible to take my eyes off this woman. I want to study every last inch of her. The light smattering of freckles across the bridge of her nose and the tops of her cheeks. Her thick auburn hair, tied up in a messy bun. The way her delicate face is so expressive, although she's far too pale right now.

I reach the trailhead, and don't want to set her down. When I arrived, there were four cars in the lot. Now, apart from my truck, there's only one – a battered old, brown station wagon that looks like it should've been replaced twenty years ago.

"I can drive you to the hospital. There isn't one in Old Hemlock Valley, but West Stoneburg is only about a half an hour away."

"Oh, it's fine," she says quickly. "I don't want to be a bother."

Setting Brooke carefully on her feet, I keep a hand on her shoulder, not quite trusting her not to lose her footing. "It's no bother. You're my patient."

Her perfect eyebrow raises on one side. "Patient?"

"Yes. Like I said: I'm a medic. I'd rather not release you until you've been properly treated. Which means warmed up and examined properly."

Watching her eyes carefully, I look for any signs of fear. Most of my patients are okay with my size and crusty demeanor, because they've known me forever. But this girl doesn't know me. For all she knows, I could be some kind of crackpot.

"I'm fine," she says again, but her resolve is weakening. "I can drive into town, check back into the hotel and take a hot bath."

My head is shaking already. "I can't let you drive in your condition. You could pass out." Softening my tone as much as I can, I begin to force a professional smile, then realize it's genuine. "I have a dozen people you can call right now if you'd like to check my references. But I think the healthiest thing we can do right now, if you're worried about the hospital expense, is to get you to my house where you can take a hot shower, drink some tea, and I can check your ribs over properly."

Am I imagining the light in her eyes? Imagining the way she looks up at me with... It's not just a smile. There's something else.

"Thank you," she says softly. "I really appreciate it."

I practically lift her into the truck, cranking the heat and wrapping a blanket around her.

As we drive to my house, I'm flooded with both worry and exhilaration. I'm an expert in picking up signals about someone's health. Injuries. Illness. Complications. Things they're hiding or are embarrassed about.

Reading women, though? I have absolutely no clue.

And yet, it feels like Brooke is interested in me, in more than a healing capacity.

The idea makes my heart race as hard and fast as the rapids.

2

———————

BROOKE

I'm accustomed to being immersed in the adventures of the books I read for work. Well, work and enjoyment, if I'm being honest. This particular real-life adventure, though? Very mixed reaction so far.

Snuggled in Jonah's coat and a thick blanket, I keep sneaking glances at the profile of the incredible man who just saved me.

He's striking. Powerful features, and deep dull green eyes that somehow hint at years of experience. His rugged jawline, wide shoulders, and sturdy frame make him look every inch the mountain man. He's hard as stone, and his chiseled features make me think of Greek statues.

Plus, in those wet jeans, I got a quick but *fabulous* glimpse of his tight ass.

He's also pretty quiet. Grumpy, even. I can tell he isn't used to being chatty. But he listens well. Listens to *me*.

Even when I was stuck in the rushing water, when the only options were to release me and hope that I could swim for it or pull me up over the rock, he let me make the choice. I mean, yes, he took control of the situation and was telling me what to do by pointing out the obvious, but he let the decision be mine.

I could feel how cautious he was being, and that every time I winced, it seemed to hurt him as well. I've never had anyone treat me with such care. Going to a stranger's home might not normally be the smartest idea, but letting Jonah help me feels like the right decision in this case.

Even though the left side of my ribs really hurt, and the chill feels like it's completely saturated my bones.

"Warm enough?" Jonah's voice is rich, and a bit scratchy. As rugged as the rest of him.

"Pretty good, thanks."

He sneaks a sideways glance at me, then grunts slightly before his foot presses down on the accelerator harder. "We'll have you inside in just a minute."

I gasp and clutch my side as we zoom up a long driveway toward a gorgeous house, kind of an upscale modern cabin, you could call it.

Jonah parks right in front of the large wraparound porch, then helps me out, carrying me inside and heading straight for the bathroom.

"Do you feel like you're steady enough for a shower? I'm worried about you getting in and out of the tub on your own."

As my fingertips brush the back of his neck, I wonder whether I really *want* to be alone. There's something about this strong, capable man that makes me want to touch him as much as possible. Or more to the point, have him touch me.

"I'm good to stand, thank you. You're right, bending up and down is probably a bad idea."

He sets me down by the door frame, and I hang onto it as he reaches down and takes off my shoes. Then he removes the blanket from my shoulders and helps me out of his jacket. "Don't move. I have an idea."

He returns in a moment with some cozy clothing, a fluffy towel, and a plastic chair. After handing me the clothes and towel he sets the chair in the large glass shower stall.

It feels like he's trying not to look at me. When he finally makes eye contact, his smile is forced. "Please leave the door unlocked, so you can holler if you need help. Don't use searing hot water, just comfortably warm until you feel somewhat normal. I'm going to make you some tea and fix us dinner." His brow furrows. "And then once you're warm, I need to examine that bruised spot."

"Okay. Thank you."

I shut the door and carefully shrug off my cold, wet clothing. Is it weird that he'd bring a stranger into his home? As I wait for the water to warm up, I realize I'm looking around the bathroom for signs of anyone else living here – specifically, a woman. Jonah wasn't wearing a wedding ring, but that doesn't mean he might not have a girlfriend.

But every product seems skewed toward a male demographic. Oat and cedar soap. A man's razor. Lemon rosemary shampoo.

I step carefully into the shower and nearly moan, the warmth is so nice. After about a minute my muscles unclench, and my teeth finally stop their intermittent chattering. I run the soap over me for a moment, then sit down, enjoying the way the warm spray is pummeling my back.

I choke back tears as it hits me all at once. *I could have died.* If I hadn't managed to kick my feet like a demon and scramble over to that rock... There was no way I would've been able to swim hard enough to make it to those logs. I would have been swept over the rapids like a crumpled newspaper blowing down the street.

Admittedly, it feels like a few of my fingertips are shredded, and my ribs are really starting to ache. But that's a small price to pay for not having my head bashed in and drowning.

After indulging in the blissful warmth for another few minutes, I get dressed, dry my hair, and shuffle out to the living room. Now that I can look at it properly, I have to admit that Jonah's house is absolutely gorgeous and looks utterly comfortable. Everything is done in earth tones and warm wood, and my eyes land on a gigantic squashy, navy couch.

"Yep. Right here." Jonah pats the couch invitingly, and when I sit he wraps one blanket around my shoulders and another around my feet. Then he hands me a large glass. "Mango orange smoothie," he explains. "It'll give you a shot of vitamin C and bring up your blood sugar quickly."

I take a sip, and grin up at him. "Tastes amazing. Is that ginger?"

"Yes. It increases circulation."

He returns to the kitchen as I giggle to myself. "I really like that a doctor still uses natural medicine," I call to him.

He returns with a cup of tea that definitely smells medicinal. "It's all chemistry – whether it's a drug, a vitamin, or an organic compound." His sexy lips curl up in a cockeyed smirk. "Plus there's the whole psychological aspect to making a patient feel comfortable. Lowering stress lowers cortisol, which helps the body heal itself faster."

"So this is all just a trick?" I take another few gulps of my smoothie. "Well, it tastes amazing, so I'll run with it."

"I should mention," he says, a whisper of tension crossing his features, "I'm not precisely a doctor."

"Well, you seem to know what you're doing."

"Oh, I do. I promise you that." He sits down next to me at

a polite distance. "I spent four years in Pre-med at university, but then I ended up in the army for several years as a medic overseas."

My eyes widen. "You didn't end up anywhere scary, did you?"

That adorable, crooked almost-smile again. "Not really. More like spots where the army was there to smooth things over after emergencies. I was a medic and patched up all kinds of minor injuries."

"So is that your job now?"

His head tilts back and forth. "Old Hemlock Valley can't afford a full-time doctor. But I don't need a day job. So, I have a small free clinic at City Hall that's open a few afternoons a week. And people know they can just show up here on my doorstep if there's an emergency. People drive down to West Stoneburg for doctors, specialists, and the hospital."

"A small town almost-doctor that works for nothing?" My grin feels unnaturally wide. "Plus you just go around randomly saving peoples' lives in the forest? You sound like a pretty good guy, Jonah."

His lips twist slightly, and I swear he might be almost blushing under that outdoorsy tan.

"Official examination time." He takes the glass from my hand, then inspects my palms and fingers. A first aid kit is under the coffee table, and he pulls it out to grab a few bandages. He disinfects and wraps the cuts on two of my fingers.

"Any dizziness, shortness of breath, joint pain...anything strange at all?"

I shake my head. "I mean, everything feels a bit tired and achy, but I assume that's from tumbling like an idiot into the river."

"Please. You're not an idiot."

"Okay, I was busy sketching the curves of the river and tripped over my own damn feet, is that better?" My heavy sigh makes him look up. "I do that a bit more than the average person."

"Luckily, you won't be moving off this couch for a good long while."

He stands up, pushing the coffee table out of the way. Then he pauses. "Brooke, I appreciate you trusting me to take care of you. Can you lie down and let me examine your ribs?"

I appreciate that he truly wants me to be comfortable. "Sure. Thank you."

I stretch out on my back, trying to stop myself from wincing as I lift my left arm. Jonah kneels beside me, and I can sense that he's reluctant to pull up the baggy sweatshirt he loaned me. So I latch my right fingertips around the bottom, pulling it up so it's still covering my breast enough to be somewhat decent.

He swallows hard and clears his throat. "Thank you." His warm hands are incredibly gentle as he pokes around my ribs with a feather-light touch. I only jump hard once.

"I'm so sorry, but I'm going to have to run my finger along that spot again to make sure there's no fracture. I will not judge you if you scream or slap me."

"All good. Go ahead." My eyes fall closed, and my breathing stops at the strange, aching pain, but I manage to say silent.

"All done," he says quickly. When I open my eyes, he's smiling. "You're brave. I like that. I hate to do this to you, but you need an ice pack for a while."

Why do I feel unbelievably proud of myself for impressing him? Why do I feel so touched at the way he pulls the shirt back down, then bundles me back in the blanket?

I've kind of sworn off men and relationships in general since I've never seen one where the woman wasn't held back and restrained. Where her life wasn't stomped over to better his.

But even though I've only known him for an hour, Jonah makes me feel treasured.

I'm already addicted to his touch. To the way he looks at me.

To the way I feel around this smart, strong, rugged stranger.

3

—————

JONAH

I shuffle around the kitchen, preparing dinner as if lost in a fog.

What the hell is wrong with me? I'm usually a clear minded person. I have tasks to accomplish, I do them, I move on. But ever since the first second I took a good look at Brooke's face, it's like my brain is full of mist.

I could barely breathe while examining her ribs, my fingertips barely an eighth of an inch from the underside of her soft, full breast.

I've examined hundreds of women in all kinds of situations, and never had that reaction. Did I do anything wildly unprofessional? No. I was still totally focused on ensuring that Brooke was okay. Well, and making sure she didn't see the front of my jeans when I stood up.

But I've already been too familiar with the sweet little stranger on my couch. That's another thing... I've treated all kinds of people at my kitchen table, but it's never occurred to me to invite anyone to stay the night.

But I simply can't let her out of my sight. Of course I'm going to use the excuse of making sure she has all the help she needs, but in truth, I just can't stomach the thought of her going home, wherever that is.

Her eyes light up when I set a plate with three small burritos in front of her. Then I bring my own dinner over, along with a bottle of painkillers, sitting what I hope is a proper distance away.

Brooke directs her smile right at me, causing that cloudy foggy feeling to overtake me again. "This looks amazing. Thank you."

"Well, you need something you can eat one-handed without cutlery. The less you use your left side, the better."

She bursts out laughing, then grimaces as she nods. "Oh wow, I see what you mean. Definitely less left side movement. The bruising is settling in, I think."

"How about just one of the painkillers, then if you don't feel better in an hour you can have a second one?"

"Perfect." She swallows the pill, as I try not to stare at her inviting pink lips. "Having my own private doctor is pretty wild. I can't thank you enough, Jonah."

I've never accepted gratitude very well. It makes me feel...prickly. All I'm doing is my job. Although in this case, it feels much more personal.

"How about you thank me by picking a movie. And after dinner I'll make up the guest room for you." Brooke takes a few bites of her burrito as I set up the TV. "You shouldn't work for several days. Any stretching or lifting is going to slow your healing. I can call your workplace if you like, so that you don't get in trouble."

Damn, I love the way this woman smiles. "It's fine. I work for myself, actually."

"Doing what?"

"I draw maps."

I blink in surprise. "Interesting. Is that why you were sketching the river?"

"Yes. Sometimes it's tricky to come up with something completely random, so I use real world examples. I feel like it just makes things more authentic."

"Wait – they aren't real maps?"

"Sometimes, yes. I'm what they call an illustrative cartographer. I take a map and customize it for the client, like I get it to match the colors and style of a presentation, or make it look antique for a book jacket, or stylized for a travel memoir."

I swallow another bite of chicken burrito. "Sounds cool."

"But then I also make fantasy maps for novelists and gamers."

I adore that she's artsy. "I've never even heard of this kind of work. How did you end up doing it?"

Brooke instinctively shrugs, then instantly regrets it, judging by the look on her face. "I did some maps in high school for history class projects and realized I had a knack for it. Then I took some online courses, posted my portfolio online, and boom – somehow I have enough freelance work these days to hold down a tiny apartment."

"That's amazing." My hand reaches out to gently squeeze her knee before I can stop myself. "I'm so proud of you for making a job out of thin air."

"Yeah, I kind of did, right?" She laughs lightly. "I'm up here on a mini vacation to do some preliminary sketches for three projects where the authors all want posters designed featuring a map of their fantasy worlds. So I headed for the mountains."

Her face falls. "Except my sketchbook went down the river, with two days' worth of work in it."

"That sucks. I'm sorry – oh, shit, what about your phone?"

"It's in my car. The battery was getting low and I was going to need the map app to get back to the hotel. It would have been too tempting to take photos when I fell into the zone, so I left it behind."

Her lovely eyes roll. "And yet I managed to get distracted anyway, when I thought I heard an animal in the woods. I wasn't watching my footing...and boom, down I went. Such a klutz."

"Do you need your phone tonight to check in with anyone?" I ask. "Will anyone be worried about you?"

My heart nearly stops as I realize that "anyone" might be a boyfriend. I desperately need Brooke to be single. I need some time to figure out how to... I sigh inwardly. To what? Make this perfect angel of a girl fall in love with me? I have no idea if that's possible, but somehow, I need to try.

"No. I told a few friends that I was leaving for a week, but we don't check on each other or anything."

"What about your family?"

Something subtle tightens her expression. "I'm not close with them."

Ouch. I definitely don't need to mention *that* again. "Okay, last question and then the interrogation is over. Where do you live?"

She finishes her first burrito, then points to the plate. "These are amazing, by the way. I live in a little apartment over the fabric shop in a place called Mackton. That's a small town near—"

"About half an hour from Oakton, right?"

"Yeah. You know it?"

"Not really know. Been through it a few times. Now, how about you pick a movie?"

Brooke narrows the selection down to a comedy or an action flick, then realizes that laughing too hard would be a bad idea. She settles on something where the British spy protagonist has some kind of super truck and a specialized weapon for every single occasion.

I just wish I had something in my mental arsenal for this occasion.

Perhaps I've been pushing it out of my mind the past several years, but I'm suddenly realizing just how truly lonely I've been. The odds of finding a woman who can handle life up here on the mountain are, as my grandfather used to say, "slim to diddly", but my experience tonight has ignited something deep within me.

Having Brooke in my home adds life to the place. More to the point, she adds life to me. It fills me with inexplicable joy to jump up and fetch her some ice cream. To set up the guest bedroom, and make sure she has everything she needs.

Caring for this incredible girl is what I've craved my entire life. It's not just the way I ache to touch her. The way I'm dying to kiss her. There's something more.

Maybe a lot more.

4

BROOKE

I'm smiling from ear to ear as I get dressed and finger comb my hair, realizing that staying here at Jonah's beautiful house feels more like a vacation than the hotel.

Not just because I am being pampered beyond belief. This is the first time I've been able to stop and take a breath in ages. Well, not literally. Breathing deeply really hurts on one side.

And being around Jonah...there's no way to describe it. Carefully pulling on his sweatshirt, I inhale the whisper of his unique masculine scent still clinging to the cotton.

I've never understood what women meant when they said a man smelled good. To me, they either smell foul if they've been sweating, or like...nothing. Maybe it's a pheromone thing. Or it's because I am wildly attracted to Jonah. Not just his gorgeous face and strong, almost hulking body.

It's the way he speaks. The habit he has of looking around when he's thinking. His organized yet overflowing bookshelf. I mean, he made a dinner that didn't require utensils so I wouldn't have to use my left arm.

What guy is that thoughtful?

It's strange. I can't quite trust it, since I've never felt like this before. But is there any reason to get my hopes up anyway? I can't quite believe an older man like him could really think of someone like me in that way.

Out in the kitchen, the fragrance of rich coffee wakes me up just as much as the fresh air blowing in the open dining room window.

"Too cold?" Jonah already looks concerned.

"Not at all, I like it. It's brisk."

He smiles, waving for me to sit down at the table. "I always feel like a shot of sunlight and fresh oxygen is the best thing first thing in the morning."

"Don't forget coffee."

He laughs, setting a tall glass of water and the bottle of painkillers in front of me. "How is the pain this morning?"

I pat my side tentatively. "It definitely aches, but it feels... stable. Does that make sense? Like, I know it's not going to get any worse, and it will probably be a lot better tomorrow."

He nods, a slight smile across his sexy lips. "That's an extremely useful assessment. I wish all patients were that descriptive."

He tips one pill into my palm. "Just to take the edge off. I'd suggest one every six hours."

I smile as he serves me breakfast sandwiches that can once again be eaten one-handed. As we eat, I pepper him with questions about Old Hemlock Valley. It sounds like an incredibly charming small town, from his vivid, detailed answers.

Jonah adores his place on the mountain; that much is

crystal clear. Somehow that balances out his slightly stoic demeanor for me, knowing that he dearly loves something.

My breath catches as his hand covers mine on the table. "I have to stop by the clinic for a couple of hours. I'm sorry. I hate the thought of leaving you alone."

"I'll be fine. I really appreciate you helping me."

"Did you have a reservation at the inn? I could drop by and close out your bill, so that you're not charged again." His eyes look even deeper green in the morning light. "That is, if you're okay staying with me a bit longer. You really shouldn't be driving for a while."

"No reservation. I called earlier and they said they had a room for one night. Until my epic fail falling into the water yesterday, I'd planned to drive to Pinesley next and stay at the little motel there. Apparently they have a quaint downtown square and an old church."

"You shouldn't be going to that town." Jonah scowls. "It's not safe for a gorgeous young lady on her own."

We both look down at the way our fingers have somehow entwined. It feels like neither of us wants to let go.

Wait. He just called me gorgeous. I'm not sure how I feel about him forbidding me to go too far away, but maybe it's his way of caring for me, and trying to keep me safe. In that case, it's sweet.

"Brooke, how old are you?" he barely breathes.

"Twenty-one. You?"

His jaw sets. "Thirty-three. Which is far too old for you, isn't it..."

That depends on what he's looking for. Since this has no chance of lasting, maybe it doesn't matter. My fingers squeeze his. "Not at all. I like that you're capable. A take charge kind of guy."

We both freeze, then our gazes gradually shift from our

hands to each other's eyes, as we realize what we've just been saying.

"Brooke, you're my patient, and..."

"No, I'm not. I'm just a clumsy girl who was incredibly lucky that a nice guy saved her."

His other hand reaches out tentatively as his fingertips graze along my collarbone before meandering into the back of my hair. My breath stutters as he gently pulls my lips to his.

Oh my...

Wow.

I had no idea.

The featherlight kiss was certainly a test to see if I'm into it. Well, I am. I reach out with my right arm circling his shoulders. As soon as Jonah realizes I've given him the green light, our kiss deepens immediately.

Fire licks up my spine as I try to make sense of the feelings radiating off him. Hunger. Raw, unbridled lust.

Jonah wants me. Badly.

I feel chilled and overheated at the same time as a vortex of new sensations swirls through me. I've had a few kisses before, but this is *nothing* like that. This is a full body tingling, savage...*claiming.*

Jonah growls into my mouth, kissing me deeper, harder, as I can feel his barely restrained passion. He's been so reserved and careful up till now that seeing this wild side of him is thrilling. What other surprises could this man have in store for me?

Just as I'm starting to think about how close his bedroom is, and how it feels like my panties are becoming steamy, he reluctantly pulls away. His hands grasp mine as he meets my eyes. "I'm sorry. I need to get to the clinic."

"I get it."

"Sit on the couch and rest. If there's a knock at the door, don't get up, just call out, okay?"

"Sure." Maybe he's expecting deliveries. I bet his parcels don't get stolen from the porch way out here like they sometimes do in Mackton.

My tiny squeal brings a smile to his lips as he lifts me up and carries me to the couch. He arranges a blanket over me, places a pillow against my side to hold me in place, and sets water, coffee, and the bottle of painkillers in front of me.

Then he writes down two phone numbers on a notepad. "The top one is my cell. The bottom one's the clinic. There's a landline in the kitchen. Where are your car keys?"

"In the pocket of my jacket."

He finds them, then gathers a few things together before changing out of his snug t-shirt into a navy button down. My bottom lip sticks out. "Awww, no fair. Now your patients can't admire that chest."

Jonah's lips fall open a second, then he clamps his mouth shut. Have I made him flustered?

"Behave." His voice is deep and growly as he heads to the door. Then he comes back to kiss my forehead. "Seriously, please rest. Take another pill in two hours. Ice your ribs for ten minutes every hour or two. And please call if you need anything at all."

"I will. Thank you."

He pauses at the door. "Don't take this the wrong way, because obviously I'm truly sorry you're hurt, but... I really like having you here, Brooke."

I really like being here, too.

In a gorgeous mountain wilderness cabin.

With a sexy man who kisses me like he never wants me to leave.

5

JONAH

My body is on autopilot as I drive to my clinic. Then it's my brain's turn as I check in with several patients, who are also neighbors.

Luckily there isn't anything complicated today. A farmer who needs half a dozen stitches. Reassuring a nervous first-time mother. Checking on a shoulder injury to make sure things are progressing well.

Everyone knows I'm not one for small talk. If I mention the weather, that's an official conversation for me, and frankly beyond the matter at hand. Most people appreciate that I get them in and out in the shortest amount of time.

But today I wish that Brooke was here so that we could chat in between visitors. What would she think of this place? Would she be interested in my work, or bored to tears?

I miss her already. What's wrong with me? It's not like a breathtaking girl like her would just drop everything to move in with a grouchy loner in the woods.

Everything feels sluggish as I scrub my hands and replace the paper on the examination table.

I can't hold Brooke back. She has her entire life ahead of her. Who knows – she might end up wanting a career that involves a lot of travel. Or being in a big city. Nobody knows what the hell they're doing at twenty-one, do they?

Although Brooke seems very steady for someone her age. Wise beyond her years, working for herself...and the way she managed to breathe and ignore her pain was admirable.

Crap, is she going to remember to ice her ribs?

I glance out the window and see my next appointment pulling into the lot. Grabbing my phone, I make a quick call before setting up my side table to remove some particularly vicious wood splinters for a local lumberjack.

By the time I'm driving home, my fingers are tense around the wheel and my foot is way too heavy on the gas. I need to find out if there's any hope for us. One way or the other, I need to know. That'll determine what steps to take next.

When I walk in the door of my house, my stress melts away as I see Brooke on the couch eating ice cream.

Her eyes narrow. "You sent someone to *check up* on me?" Brooke's expression is indignant annoyance, despite her soft laughter. The laughter stops abruptly as she puts down the spoon and clutches her ribs. "Crap."

"Yes, I did." I rush to her side. "Did you take another pain killer?"

"No." She points to the ice pack wrapped in a towel on the coffee table. "Your minion insisted that I put cold on it for ten minutes." Her eyes light up with a smile. "Clark was adamant that I didn't get any ice cream until I obeyed."

"Good." I hand her a pill and some water. "You're supposed to take these regularly. That way the pain won't get too bad."

She swallows, then rolls her lovely eyes. "I've always tried to take the bare minimum of pills."

"This really is the bare minimum for an injury like this." Taking her hands, I sit close. My heart pounds as she shifts to press her right side against me. "Unless you *want* to suffer?"

She pouts dramatically. "Of course not."

"Do you want to be well enough tomorrow to come to work with me?"

Damn. The way her eyes light up sends blood hammering through my veins and...elsewhere.

"Really?"

"Only if you're better." My head tips toward the window. "By the way, your car is parked out front."

"What? How did you manage that?"

"My younger brother Josh drove it here, then hitched a ride back to his place with Clark."

Brooke squeezes my fingers. "So there's a whole club of helpful mountain men around here?"

"More like an odd assortment of family, and people we've known so long that they might as well be family. Do you need anything from your car?"

Brooke runs through a list of items, and I bring them inside, taking most of them to the guest room. Then I set a bag on the coffee table. "To replace your sketchbook that fell in the river. There isn't a huge selection at the local bookstore, but Janice said these were good for pencil drawings."

She flinches as she tries to lean forward, so I take out the two sketchbooks for her plus a large tin of fancy pencils. Her perfect lips fall open. "You... You got me the full Staedtler set? I was saving up for that."

"I asked for her recommendation, and this is what she told me to get."

"Thank you, Jonah. This is amazing."

Brooke's expressive gray eyes stare up at me, and I feel something shift in my lower belly. This incredible woman has never had anyone be sweet with her. I can feel it. That's why the simplest gesture means so much to her.

It blows my mind, makes me sad and sends rage simmering through me all at once. The entire world should be sweet to this incredible girl.

Once she's mine, I'll make sure that happens.

The decision has been made.

6

BROOKE

I've always been pretty shy around guys, but Jonah is different. I'm fluttery when he's around, but it's only partly nerves.

The way he looks at me, studies me so meticulously... It's as if he's suddenly dedicating his entire life to figuring me out.

And *I love it.*

Having his complete attention on me makes me feel like I'm lighting up from within. It's also drawing my focus to areas of my body I hadn't really thought about sharing with anyone else until I found someone really special.

Like Jonah.

He obviously has some sort of shell around him, but whenever he touches me, the shell cracks a little, and I see something different in his eyes.

I'm so touched that he sent his friend Clark over to bring me ice cream and make sure I was using an ice pack. And the new sketchbooks, and the Staedtler pencils?

I'm positive that it's his way of letting me know that he

really likes me and doesn't just think of me as some random weird girl he yanked out of the river.

Jonah busies himself in the kitchen, making yet another wonderful one-handed dinner of hummus wraps this time. We eat together on the couch, watching another movie – a sci-fi mystery, his pick, with a cheesy plot but unbelievable special effects.

About halfway through, he casually stretches his thick arm around my shoulders, then glances over to make sure I'm okay with it. My right side snuggles directly against him, and I wonder how much of a green light he's going to need to go any further.

When I'm getting ready for bed, he encourages me to take another painkiller both to keep the swelling down and to make sure that I don't wake up uncomfortable in the night.

"Tomorrow we can start you with heating pads," he says. "Then it should start improving more quickly."

"I'm okay, really."

His eyebrow lifts. "I've been watching the way you move. Your entire side is stiff."

The remark raises a tiny prickle in the back of my shoulders. I slip into the guest room bed, patting the edge for him to sit down. He hesitates, then sits as far away as he can. "What do you mean, studying my movements? Why?"

Jonah actually looks uncomfortable, staring down at his hands. "Just keeping an eye on you. If you get worse, or aren't progressing as fast as I'd like, we need to get you to the hospital."

Reaching out, I take his hand and squeeze it. "I appreciate that you're taking such wonderful care of me, but it's really not that bad."

"It's the very least I can do after hurting you."

I bop him on the nose. "Excuse me? You didn't hurt me. You saved me."

He takes my hand again. "This is kind of a weird situation, Brooke. You're pretty much stuck out here with me. And I don't want you to think...I mean, I'm not the kind of guy who..."

The poor guy. I need to find a way to let these physical feelings out. "You said that you believe in natural remedies, right?"

"Yeah. Why?"

Lifting both of our hands, I point to my mouth. "Do you believe that kissing someone better makes the pain go away?"

Once again, it's as if I flipped a switch.

He moves slowly, as if he's afraid to speed up. His strong hands move me gently until I'm lying back on the pillow. Then he stretches out beside me, brushing my hair from my cheek before bringing his lips to mine.

Fireworks.

His delicate, sweet, tentative kiss turns into an explosion of passion in about twenty seconds.

I can hardly breathe from the way his mouth devours mine as his left arm scoops under to cradle my body against his. Every time I let out a soft moan, I can feel him smile against my lips.

He loves that he drives me crazy.

His right hand latches around my hip, tilting me toward him. Everything is beginning to tingle, my skin feeling overheated, my pulse ragged as I realize I'm finally in bed with a man. No, not just a man. The sexiest mountain man I've ever seen.

And he seems to be truly hungry for me.

I hear a dark growling scrape at the back of his throat as his fingers thread into the back of my hair, his other hand loosening my shirt and gliding up my spine. Then he freezes for a second.

"Yes," I whisper. "Whatever you're thinking, yes."

That's all it takes for him to start caressing my back, then move his hand around to the front. He carefully avoids my ribs, going straight from my trembling stomach to my breast.

Jonah touches me confidently, his large, warm palms gliding over my skin, sending sparks of desire through every inch of my body. I never knew my nipples were so directly connected to the spot between my thighs that's already becoming wet and open.

I want him.

I've never had these thoughts about a man. Not with this level of intensity. No matter how far he wants to go, I already know I won't be stopping him. I can't. My curiosity has taken over and is making secret backroom deals with my libido to keep my sense of logic out of the negotiation.

Jonah slips his left arm under me, immobilizing me so that I can't squirm and hurt my ribs before hitching up my shirt to admire my breasts.

My stomach flutters as his thumb caresses my nipple while he kisses me gently again. As my fingers thread into the back of his hair, I keep my left hand on the bed so I don't move too much and make him nervous.

I moan softly as his palm drifts down my belly, feeding his hunger. His fingertips toy with the top edge of my baggy old yoga pants, and he pulls back to look into my eyes.

"I need to watch you come." The raw hunger in his low tone sends shivers up the backs of my legs. "I won't let you move around too much and hurt yourself. Do you trust me?"

"Yes."

The word has barely passed my lips when I gasp, feeling the pressure of his big, heavy hand against my mound, already slipping into my panties.

I guess it makes sense that a medic, as an expert on human anatomy, would know exactly how to touch a woman. But it feels like Jonah knows exactly how to touch *me* personally. His fingertips gently part my folds as my legs fall open. He inhales sharply when we both realize how wet I am. My entire body begins to tremble as his fingers glide softly in and around my sensitive skin, exploring, watching every reaction I make.

"Relax." His voice has turned darker. Gravelly. "You're not supposed to move, remember? If you pull your side, it'll take longer to heal."

Honestly, I don't think I'd mind staying if he kept doing this.

My breathy gasp as the blunt end of his finger notches inside me makes him chuckle. "So sensitive. And how about *this*?" My breath becomes halting and fluttery as he gently circles around my clit, then flicks straight across the surface.

My thighs tighten, my left hand gripping the sheet under me as the right tangles in his hair, probably pulling too tightly.

"So beautiful," he murmurs, kissing along my cheekbone, then my jawline. Somehow he manages to stroke gently through my crease with two fingers, while the center one brushes and taps at my clit.

Everything pulls inward, tensing up and trembling, and I realize I'm about to come unbelievably hard. I have no idea what's going to happen when I do. Gazing into his stunning deep eyes, I have a feeling that I could do anything right now. As long as I'm happy, he's happy. What would it feel like to satisfy him? To make him feel everything I'm feeling now?

Just the thought of having his huge, hard cock in my hand, never mind anywhere else, sends me over the edge. My mouth falls open with a weak cry, and then Jonah crushes his mouth to mine, kissing me, devouring me as he caresses my clit, his other finger nudging inside me just enough to make me feel slightly full. I swear I see stars and tiny blue lights as the pulsing wave of raw sensation powers through me.

I hear a gritty growl in the back of his throat. "So sexy. Sweet and beautiful and hot."

I've never once thought of myself as hot. Yet Jonah makes me feel that way. Sensual. Sexual. So many things that I've never felt before.

He kisses me gently again, then pulls his hand out of my underwear and slips his middle finger between his lips, his eyes falling closed. "Mmm. I knew you'd taste delicious."

The look in his eyes is so dreamy. I was wondering if a sexy older man alone in the woods might think of a young lady on her own as some kind of opportunity for a little fling.

But the look in his eyes stops that idea in its tracks. He wants me. Possibly for a lot longer than I could have imagined.

Jonah shuffles my clothing back in place, then tucks me into bed with a pillow wedged against my left side to keep me from rolling onto it.

He kisses my forehead. "I'd love to have you in my bed tonight, gorgeous, but I know that we'd end up snuggling, and tonight you need deep sleep, and to keep your ribs as still as possible. Okay?"

"You're right. Thanks."

He leans in again for another soft, sweet kiss that makes me tingle all the way to the tips of my toes. After he turns off the light and shuts the door, I stifle a giggle.

Does he really think I could fall asleep right after that?

7

JONAH

The next day, I find myself driving more slowly than usual on the way to the clinic. I don't want Brooke to miss a thing.

She looks delighted by the scenery around us, staring out at the trees and occasional rocky outcrops while sipping on her traveler coffee mug.

Every time she picks up the mug, I'm pleased to notice she's carefully keeping her left side immobilized. I managed to get her to take another painkiller this morning, but she only grudgingly obliged. I slow down to a crawl as we reach a particularly sharp turn that I know will cause her to lean to the left.

I've never been able to stand seeing people in pain, even though I know the five minutes of discomfort while getting stitches will speed healing and decrease pain later. Or that the uncomfortable operation might save someone's life.

My mind keeps debating what I can safely do to relieve her pain completely. Muscle relaxants would make her too loose, and she might inadvertently pull that area more. Too many painkillers will make her groggy, which could make her clumsy. Ice and rest were all I could do for the first day and a half, but today is all about heat therapy.

We drive through the center of town, and Brooke perks up as she looks around at the various businesses. Fran's Diner, Jim's Pizza, Corina's Coffee. The bookstore, the library, and Tidy's Department Store. It's not a large town by any stretch of the imagination, but we have all of the basics covered.

"A department store?" she asks, wide-eyed. "What, did we time travel back to the sixties?"

"Sort of. That's when this area had a bit of a population boom."

I pull into the back of City Hall, and Brooke's eyes get even wider. "This one building holds the town council, the police, *and* the medical clinic?"

"Yes. My great-grandfather had this building constructed, and wanted it to be large enough to suit the town for a very long time."

"So your family has been on Wolfe Mountain for... Well, I guess your family is why it's even called Wolfe Mountain?"

"Exactly. My great-grandfather Adler Wolfe came over from Europe and settled here. He came here to buy up cheap land. Many people thought the mountain was too harsh, so he was able to purchase huge swaths of it."

I love how Brooke is listening so attentively, as if she's taking notes.

"Adler had two kids; one was my grandfather Spencer. Spencer had four sons, one of whom was my father Carver. I have two younger brothers, Jace and Josh, and a buttload of cousins. Everyone had large families and spread out across the forest." I park, then dart around to help Brooke out of the truck. "People joke that the Wolfes breed more than the rabbits around here."

She laughs, then I feel her fingers tighten on my arm.

Locking her eyes with mine, I place my palm in the center of her back. "Tell me honestly, Brooke. Please. How much does that hurt?"

There's a long pause as her blinking slows down.

"I can almost hear you thinking," I say softly. "You don't want to lie to me. You also don't want to tell the truth and let me know how much it hurts. Am I right?"

She sighs. "It's just, you know. Uncomfortable."

"On a scale of one to ten, is the pain above a two?"

Her lips press together for a moment. "I've never understood that question. Like, my scale might be different than yours."

My faint growl makes her smile. "Humor me. Today's going to be all about your healing. Got it?"

She glowers, even though her eyes are dancing. "We're here to heal your patients."

"Precisely. And you are my most important patient. So you must follow your not-really-a-doctor's orders."

We walk inside, and I keep my arm around her until she tries to pull away. "Isn't this a little unprofessional?" she asks.

"That didn't even occur to me. I have no problem with anyone knowing that we are..." Shit. We haven't even begun to talk about this. What are we, anyway?

"Um...at the beginning of...whatever we're at the beginning of?" she offers, quirking up an eyebrow.

I get the impression that she's uncomfortable with defining things so soon. Strange. Most women want a committed relationship, or so I've heard. But if that's what the lady wants, that's what the lady gets. "Exactly."

Once we're inside, I get Brooke organized with water, juice, a fresh coffee, and a massive heating pad wrapped around her ribs as she lounges in the easy chair in the waiting room. Then I set a canvas bag with her sketching supplies beside her.

She sighs. "I feel like a helpless, broken princess."

I hand her another painkiller. "It would make me very happy if we increased the dose a bit today, plus applied heat, and have you really promise not to move around much. This is probably going to be the worst day for you, and all that will take the edge off."

"Fine." She washes the pill down with juice. "Can I at least pretend I'm your receptionist today so I don't feel so useless?"

"Can you do that without moving a muscle?"

She points to her mouth. "Okay, not receptionist, more like official greeter. All talking, no moving."

Drawing my attention to her perfect lips makes me bend down to kiss her gently. I jump away as the door opens.

Brooke doesn't miss a beat, smiling up at Mr. Cabrido. "Good morning, sir. Welcome to the clinic."

The elderly gentleman's eyes grow wide, but he smiles. "Good... Good morning, miss."

I wave him into the exam room, leaving Brooke grinning to herself.

Luckily, my appointments today are nothing more than the usual routine of determining who should go to West Stoneburg for further tests or x-rays, and who is okay to rest up at home for several days.

Just as I'm saying goodbye to a preteen boy and his nervous mother, assuring them it's a slight goose egg, not a full on concussion, I hear Brooke's voice. "Jonah! Emergency!" I race out to the waiting room with my heart in my throat, only breathing again when I see that Brooke is fine.

She's gesturing to a local farmer whose hand is wrapped in several bloody rags. "No big deal," Ernest mutters, shaking his head. "Might need a stitch or two, though."

A quick examination determines that in fact he needs over a dozen stitches, all the way up the outside of his wrist and arm. "It's long, but luckily it isn't deep. No tendons or nerves affected," I assure him.

"Yeah, just a big ol' bloody mess. Sorry to trouble you with this, doc."

"Nonsense. It's what I'm here for."

As I set to work, I notice Brooke is standing in the doorway. Her eyes are wide as she looks at Ernest. "Can I get you anything?" she asks gently. "Stitches are no fun. If you need a coffee, or someone to chat and distract you, perhaps I can help."

Ernest chuckles, smiling widely. "That's mighty nice of you, miss. You know, I wouldn't mind a coffee. I kicked mine over when this darn thing happened. Black, please and thank you."

As I stare into Brooke's lovely gray eyes, I realize I'm already in love with her. She's ignoring her own pain to help a perfect stranger. Trying to help, no matter what. Not only is that the mark of a good person, it's a quality people need to survive up here on the harsh mountain.

Maybe...just maybe... It's a sign.

8

BROOKE

I think Jonah was impressed that I sat with Ernest over coffee while his arm was being stitched up, chatting about the ins and outs of repairing your own tractor.

Good. I want to show him that I can be useful. He seems more than delighted to spoil me rotten, which I appreciate, but I don't want him to think for one second that I expect that. I've always looked out for myself. Always had to.

Plus, I know that the whole Jonah caring for me thing is simply a temporary fantasy, certainly not something that would last. Although I can't stop thinking about how amazing it would be to try. Maybe. Is there even the smallest chance that I could move up here, find a little apartment, and date Jonah for a while?

Although he probably wouldn't be interested after he saw where I came from. After he found out how my father treated my mother, and how I've been trying to keep my distance from her my entire life.

I mean, come on. Jonah comes from a wealthy family with well-established roots. His ancestors basically built this town, for crying out loud! There's no way he could be seen with someone like me. I have no real family; there's nothing notable about me. My "career", if you wanted to be generous and call it that, is drawing pretend maps for strangers online. Not really something normal people would build a life around.

Plus... I can't quite tell how controlling Jonah is. He knows what I need to do to heal these stupid bruised ribs, so I know he's not trying to be bossy there, and just wants the best for me. And yet, part of me wants to rebel anyway. What's up with that? Maybe I'm just prickly because I really do need his help right now, plus I'm in pain.

I assist him all day long, trying to prove myself. Not just to him, but also to that creepy little negative voice in the back of my mind questioning that I could even think about belonging here in Old Hemlock Valley. It's a charming town with lovely people. The kind of place I've always dreamed of living.

When we get into Jonah's truck at the end of his shift, he asks, "How did your sketching go today between patients?"

"Amazing, actually. I think I've decided on the style I'm going to use for one client, and the other two are just the same as before, with a few minor adjustments. It should all come together pretty soon."

"That's great. Hey, how do you feel about picking up some burritos?"

"Only if you'll let me treat."

His shifty side eye tells me that's not an option. "That's very sweet, but it's on me."

"*Grrr.*"

My pathetic attempt at a fierce growl makes him chuckle. "You know, I've laughed more with you in the past few days than I have in years."

Reaching out to squeeze his knee, I laugh with him. "Me too."

"Hey, your side is a bit better, right?"

"Yeah – it is, actually."

"Amazing. Heating pads, rest and more painkillers. It's almost like I know what I'm talking about."

I hate that his overprotective instincts were correct. "*Grrr.*"

We drive to a quaint old-fashioned diner called Fran's. It has the typical black and white checkered floor, vinyl booths, and older waitresses who call you "Sugar". But the menu isn't your typical fifties fare, extending beyond burgers to burritos to pasta.

We order from their take-out menu and sit in a booth for the ten minutes it takes them to prepare our food.

The decor gets us chatting about retro movies, but my eyes keep darting around the room as we talk. "What is it?" Jonah reaches across the table to take my hand. "Something making you jumpy?"

"Not really. It just occurred to me that probably within the next hour every single person in town is going to be talking about you walking in here with your arm around some strange girl."

Jonah shoots a look over his shoulder and a half dozen sets of eyeballs swivel back to their plates. "For the record, I don't think you're strange. Delightfully quirky? Maybe."

My fingers squeeze his. "You know what I mean. I'm not from around here. An outsider. Small-town people hate outsiders, right?"

He smiles, his dark eyes pulling me in with a magnetism that feels otherworldly. "Not here. There's no hate in this town." His thumb caresses the side of my hand. "Some extra questions, maybe. But just part of the getting-to-know-you process."

I don't know how to answer that, so I simply nod.

"For the record," he murmurs softly, "I'm really enjoying the getting-to-know-you process." He picks up my hand, kissing the back of it right there in front of several white-haired women who are very obviously staring.

"Looking forward to getting you home, gorgeous," he says softly, leaning in to kiss my cheek before standing to pick up our order.

Great. Now, all of Old Hemlock Valley is going to think that Jonah has a girlfriend. I want it to be true. So much. But I guess I want to know all the details before I jump in with both feet.

Before it's too late for me to jump back out, if I need to.

9

___

JONAH

Brooke rolls her eyes when I bundle her up on the couch in a blanket and a heating pad before I will allow her to eat dinner. It feels like she's getting a little frustrated at my overprotectiveness, but at least she's still laughing about it. I'd rather annoy her slightly than delay her healing.

I wait until she's taken a few bites before handing her a painkiller, which she accepts with another exaggerated eye roll. I'm not sure if she's aware of how carefully I've been timing her pills all day, giving her just enough to keep her from wincing and walking too stiffly, but not enough to make her the slightest bit groggy.

I've been observing her reaction time just to be sure. Unobtrusive things like darting my head to the left as if I've seen a bird flit past the window, and noting how long it takes her to look as well. Or when I pass her something, making sure there's no delay in her motor functions.

I've always been very observant with my patients. Many of them lie about their levels of pain or try to hide injuries. Especially if their spouse is there.

Hell, I had one guy who raises horses come in because his wife was concerned about his sprained ankle. It wasn't until he tried to open the door for them to leave that I spotted his broken wrist. He hadn't wanted to bother me with it, figuring it would just take a few days to "shake off".

There's no way I'm going to allow Brooke to be in pain if I can help it. It actually hurts me to think she might be uncomfortable.

By the end of our after-dinner movie, we're sitting with her legs stretched across my lap, casually cuddling. She turns to me with an adorable smile. "You know, I've been rolling my eyes at your fussiness, but the heating pad really does help. Check it out." Her left arm stretches in a slow circle forward, then up and back as if she were doing the backstroke.

"That's great, I'm glad." I take her hand in mine to prevent her from doing it again and fix her with a stare. "But the whole immobilization thing means that you don't stretch like that very much."

"*Grr.*"

There's something about her adorable soft growls of annoyance that makes my pulse...and other things...surge. I'm at least half hard every time she's in my arms, but now, with the way she snuggles against me, her knee brushing across the front of my pants...

I've never wanted a woman like this. No, not want. *Need.* For the first time in my life, this Wolfe really feels like an actual wolf, wanting to stalk and capture my prey. Yet here she is already in my arms, those big, soft gray eyes staring up at me as if she already knows exactly what I want.

I should not be this hard, with my long-neglected cock pulsing in my jeans. I should not be thinking of making her cry out like she did last night, coming so sweetly in my hand.

Swallowing hard, I clear my throat. "Coffee? Or maybe herbal tea?"

She fists the front of my t-shirt, pulling me closer. "Ah-ah-ah. I'm pretty sure you were thinking about something else two seconds ago. What was it?"

"It's much too soon to be thinking like that."

"Says who? I thought one of the perks of being a wild mountain man was that you lived by your own rules and all that good stuff. Right?"

"I guess you might have a point."

Our lips meet softly, and the gentle kiss is all it takes to ignite our desire. Her sensual mouth moves against mine, opening to help me delve deeper, the kiss taking on a life of its own.

I shove the coffee table out of the way with my foot, holding her against me as I gently roll onto the floor. I stretch out with Brooke on top of me, my hands now free to caress her back, her voluptuous ass, the back of her thighs. Everywhere.

Her tongue dances with mine as her body weight settles over me. The rush of possessiveness is mind-blowing. This precious girl already means so much to me. I can't possibly do the gentlemanly thing and wait any longer.

"I want to see you naked, gorgeous." I feel her shiver at my murmured request. Or was it a command? Either way, she nods.

I help her carefully slip off her tank top and long sleeve t-shirt together. Then I roll her gently onto her back on the thick carpet, shoving the coffee table further away. Her auburn hair fanned out against the forest green area rug is so beautiful that it makes me want to take a photo of her in this perfect moment.

Maybe next time.

She lifts her hips as I pull down her yoga pants, and I'm relieved to notice that she doesn't flinch when moving her side slightly.

It feels like I can already read her, that I can tell what she needs, but I'm not going to make any assumptions, just in case.

Staring at her pale, delicate skin stretched out underneath me, my breath is ragged. "Luscious," I growl, as my palms coast up her thighs, spreading them apart. "Can I lick your sweet little pussy? I'll be so nice and slow, promise."

Brooke looks deeply into my eyes, like she's lost for a moment. Then she nods. "Please."

Remembering what she said last night, I pull off my t-shirt and toss it behind me. I have to admit to a certain bit of self-satisfaction as I watch her eyes drift hungrily across my chest. "How is a medic built like a lumberjack?" she whispers as I settle between her thighs.

"I have lots of lumberjacking to do on my own property," I say with a chuckle. "Plus there's a really good gym in town."

I don't mention that the gym is a great place to blow off steam if you haven't been with a woman in years, and have a lot of pent up...*energy.*

I kiss an arc from hip bone to hip bone. Brooke's knees bend up slightly as I spread her wide, my warm breath whispering across her delicate skin. Her pussy is perfect – pink and fresh and sinfully sweet. My fingers are already caressing her, my tongue gliding straight through her crease as she gasps, her nipples tightening immediately. As I pull her clit between my lips, I reach a hand up to fondle her breast, grazing her nipple with my thumb until her head rolls back.

"Look at me." I don't know why my voice is so dark. "Look into my eyes, baby. Let me see you come." She nods, then giggles when I rub the scruff of my beard against her inner thigh.

Brooke looks like an offering stretched out on the dark rug, her pale skin luminous, her curvy figure undulating slightly. As I plunge my tongue deep inside her, she lets out a low hoarse "Oh!" Then she sighs contentedly. "Wowww..."

My fingers tease at her sensitive peaks, her breasts growing warm under my left hand as I alternate back and forth. My right fingertips are busy gliding in and around her soft folds, listening to her breath hitch as I explore every sensitive nook. My thumb grazes her clit and she gasps, her shoulders lifting up and forward as she grips the top of my hair. I'm happy to see she doesn't wince in the slightest.

I meet her eyes, silently encouraging her to pull and push me in whatever direction she pleases. As soon as she begins to pull me closer, I feel her juices begin to flood my tongue.

Her thighs tighten around my shoulders, ankles crossing behind my back as her body closes in. "Delicious," I groan. "That's it. Come on my tongue, baby. Let me feel you. Please."

"Yeah," she moans softly. "It's... so..." She loses her train of thought as I trace around her clit gently, then bump my thumb flat against the sensitive point.

"Hot," I growl into her soaking pussy. "That's what it is. Hot, and sexy as hell."

Her fingers tighten in my hair, and I feel the prick of her fingernails against my scalp. "Mmm," I groan, feeling how close she is. Realizing that my gorgeous girl is hovering right at the point of no return and that I brought her there is wildly satisfying to me.

I hum again, plunging my tongue as deep as it will go, fucking her with it as my thumb bears down, rubbing her clit in tight little circles. Brooke's eyes blaze, her mouth falling open, then she cries out, frantically clutching at me as her entire body trembles.

It's the sexiest thing in the world to feel her ankles shaking against my back. Her pussy dripping on my lips. Her fingers spearing through my hair as I pull every drop of bliss from my beautiful woman's body.

After she stops twitching, she lies back, looking almost sheepish.

"So beautiful," I murmur. She looks lost and vulnerable now, naked and satiated, but perhaps also nervous about what's next.

I kiss my way up her body, paying special attention to her nipples before lying beside her, propped up on my elbow.

"That was amazing," she breathes.

"The important thing is, did you pull your side at all?"

She smirks. "Grr. *No.*"

"Do you think that lying here flat on the floor is the best place for healing, or should I pick you up and take you to my bed?"

Brooke's eyes dance. "You know, I think a small amount of movement might be good for me. Maybe if we snuggled in your bed for a while, it would help me heal?"

My thumb drags across her bottom lip. "Definitely snuggle."

Sometimes when Brooke is thinking, her eyes twinkle and her lips pull to the side in an adorable cross between a smirk and a smile. "Except, since I'm all naked, I might get cold..."

"Are you saying you might need a heating pad?"

"I'm saying I might need"...her hand trails slowly from my collarbone down my chest, then down my abs..."you to be naked as well. You're very warm."

Leaning in, I breathe against her ear, "if we're both naked, I'm going to get very filthy and inappropriate ideas."

Her chin tips up and down immediately. "Good. Those are the kinds of ideas I want you to be having right now."

I scoop her up quickly, cradling her against my chest so there's no pressure on her side.

After just two steps toward the bedroom, my cock feels like it's going to burst just from looking at the incredible woman in my arms. No matter what happens, I already know that this is the hottest night of my life.

It feels like Brooke was sent to me. The dream woman I've always longed for. The partner I've always needed. It's too soon, and the ideas are too big, but sometimes when you know, you know.

Brooke is the one for me.

Assuming, of course, that she wants to become a mountain woman.

And assuming I can figure out how to be the right man for her.

10

BROOKE

Whenever I've read about people having an out of body experience, I've always thought it sounded a bit far-fetched. Now, as Jonah carries me to his bedroom and sets me down across the comforter, I genuinely feel like I'm floating several feet in the air. He doesn't just admire my body, he treasures it. As he smooths my hair across the pillow, kissing my breasts and caressing my legs, I feel like a prize he has won. Cherished. *Adored.*

How can there be so much emotion in his stunning dark green eyes when we've only known each other a few days?

"I have a confession to make." His voice is always deep and gruff, as if he usually only uses it for stern, curt communication. Now it's even lower. There's also no missing the rather extreme situation going on in the front of his jeans.

"Yeah?"

"It's been so long that any condoms I had lying around are long expired. So—"

"Oh. Um. I'm on the pill. My friends were paranoid and talked me into it, and I like being able to schedule—"

He cuts me off with a kiss that takes my breath away. It feels like he's trying to consume me, trying to fuse us together into one body. He spreads my thighs, allowing him to stroke and caress my pussy lightly until I start to tremble again. His thick finger drags inside me, gathering up my moisture, then spreading it all over my swollen button.

Showers of sparks dance through my nervous system as I think about what's about to happen. My right hand darts out, fumbling to undo his jeans.

"Is this what you want?" He studies my face intently.

"Yes."

My next exhale shudders as his finger glides inside me. His brows knit together slightly. "You're very tight. Are you..." I nod.

"Yes. But I want to do this. I want..." My thoughts slow down, as I realize how unbelievably sexy this moment is. "I want you," I finally whisper.

His lips barely brush mine, then I moan as he jumps up to standing.

I watch in awe as he strips off his jeans and shorts, leaving him gloriously naked. My eyes aren't big enough to take him all in. He really is built like a lumberjack – thick, sculpted shoulders. Hard slabs of muscle across his chest. Defined abs, and two perfect arcing lines over his hips.

I'll have to study the rest of him later, since the massive erection pointing straight at me seems like it needs my attention urgently.

My hand darts out, grasping the tip gently. I have no idea what I'm doing, but his sharp inhale as I begin to stroke down to the base tells me I must be doing something right. His stomach and thighs tighten as I begin to stroke up and down, curling my fingers around his length as I grasp him firmly.

After a moment, a shudder goes through him, then he pulls himself from my grip, his huge, warm, masculine body taking up most of the bed as he lays down beside me.

"That felt amazing, baby." His hand gravitates to my pussy again. This time he carefully presses two fingers inside me. "Is this where you want me? Are you ready?"

He's expecting me to be timid. And although I usually am, there's no doubt or gray areas here for me. Gripping the back of his hair, I pull his lips to mine for a deep, almost frantic kiss. "Yeah," I moan against his lips. "I think I've been ready from the first time you looked into my eyes like that."

A slow smile spreads across his gorgeous face. "I swear, you're the only woman who can make me almost blush. That's the sweetest thing anyone's ever said to me, gorgeous."

The instep of my foot runs up and down his calf as I kiss him again, this time trying to make him realize how much I need him. It really is a need. And one I've ignored for too long.

Warmth blooms along my spine as he begins to roll on top of me. He feels like a bit of a predator in the way he eyes me, then nips at my throat. My breath feels stuck, my heart pounding so hard that my system is already overloaded.

"Try to relax." His voice rumbles against my skin as his lips glide along my collarbone. Somehow he manages to settle over me without crushing me, his weight distributed perfectly as my legs fall open for him.

He smiles at my surprised gasp as the weight of his long, thick cock falls against my open pussy. "You know I'll always be gentle with you, Brooke."

"I know." I leave my left hand flat on the bed so that he doesn't complain about me moving my side. The right hand stretches up around his shoulder to caress the back of his neck.

He hums blissfully. "I love when you touch me, baby."

The word love almost makes me flinch. It's too big. Too important. I have to keep reminding myself that this is just for fun and exploration. Even though I desperately want it to be more, much more, I know better than to get my hopes up too high.

The thick shaft of his cock drags up and down through my wet pussy lips, making both of us shiver. As he strokes slowly up and down, I can feel everything inside me shifting, getting ready. As if parts of me I've never paid attention to instinctively know already what's about to happen.

Jonah's dark growl fills me with lust as the thick, velvety head of his cock notches inside me. "You already feel so good around me, gorgeous," he breathes. "Want a bit more?"

Nodding, my fingers tighten, my hips lifting as my body tries to work him deeper inside. All my usual clumsiness is gone right now. Every part of me knows exactly what to do.

It feels like we can read each other's minds, knowing exactly when he wants me to lift, or when I need him to press deeper. I love the way he nudges into me so gently, his slow, careful strokes helping me adjust to his impressive girth.

The deep, primal sensation of being stretched causes me to release a breathless moan. Jonah watches my eyes carefully. "Too much?"

I grin, shaking my head, then give the back of his leg an encouraging tap with my heel.

"So tight and wet." His voice is nearly a grunt. "My beautiful artist, with her legs wrapped around me. So fucking sexy, baby."

My thighs wind around his waist more tightly, pulling

him deeper until he finally hits bottom inside me, and we both moan. "You're so perfect, Brooke," he murmurs as he kisses across my forehead.

I don't know about that, but I do love the sensation of him moving inside me with long, deep thrusts. "Oh!" I gasp. "That's a good oh, by the way," I pant immediately afterward. "In case you were wondering."

It feels like he's almost making a scooping motion with his hips, grinding hard and deep even as he moves slowly. Then his speed increases gradually, his eyes half hooded as he stares at my lips, my breasts, then down to where his huge cock is disappearing inside me.

He buries his fingers in the back of my hair, bringing my mouth to his. Then he reaches between us, spreading my pussy lips and changing his angle so the base of his shaft rubs against my clit with every stroke. Moaning into his mouth, I'm stunned by how incredible this feels. There are no words. No thoughts. Just pure sensation.

Plus a few stray emotions, like how I think I'm already falling for this incredible man.

It feels so good to be controlled this way. It's not like he's just using me for his own pleasure. It's more that Jonah knows everything that needs to happen, and is making sure that it does.

It gives me a sense of relief and release to let him take charge, and before I realize what's going on, the orgasm slams into me. Screaming into his mouth, my hips are swirling as if trying to pull him even deeper inside me while he pounds into my soaking pussy, hard and fast.

"That's it." His voice is a rasping scrape, granite on steel. "Give it to me, gorgeous. Take all of my cock. That's it..." Just as the climax grows so intense I think I might faint, his fingers tighten on me as his hips thrust forward hard, holding himself deep inside me with a choked groan, flooding my pussy with his liquid heat.

It feels like his thick shaft is pulsing inside me, and as I see the utter surrender in his eyes, I come again.

"That's it, my beautiful girl." Jonah possesses my mouth again, kissing me as if he wants the entire world to know that he's claiming me.

That's what this feels like. It's not just fun, sexy times. It's as if his body wants to bond itself to mine. As if our physical selves are in control, not our minds.

I had no idea I loved being controlled in the bedroom like this. Having a gorgeous hulking man take charge of my body and my pleasure.

As I drift off to sleep, floating on a sea of happy endorphins, it's almost possible to block out the lingering negative thoughts.

Jonah won't want to control me *all* the time, will he? He's got kind of a control freak job. Plus, he's a bit of a community leader around here. Does that mean that everyone in town will analyze our relationship? What would that mean for us if we tried to make it long-term?

Am I strong enough to draw boundaries, or am I already being swept away by this powerful mountain man?

11

———————

JONAH

I wake up feeling completely content.

Having Brooke in my world gives everything more purpose. Making coffee, fixing breakfast, loading the dishwasher. Every mundane daily task isn't simply the routine of my life anymore. It's a way of making everything perfect for her. Making her comfortable. Making sure she has everything she needs.

As I steadfastly refuse her help tidying the kitchen after a long chatty breakfast, I can see in her eyes that she's tired of being babied. Which means she'll definitely be annoyed if I leave her here at the house and send anyone to check on her again.

"Would you like to come with me to the clinic again this morning?" I ask. "I was thinking of making sandwiches and bringing them there for lunch."

"I thought you only ran the clinic in the afternoons?"

"Usually, yes. But it's the first Thursday of the month. Mrs. Jackson likes to bring her mother in at eleven-thirty so they can have their fancy lunch in town afterward." I flash Brooke a wink. "Ever since her mother hit ninety-three, Mrs.

J's become a little paranoid. She likes to bring her in often, just in case."

Brooke grabs my hand, giving it a squeeze. "That's so sweet of you to give her a special monthly mini check-up."

I shrug. "It keeps them from driving all the way to West Stoneburg and pestering the doctors there for a ton of unnecessary tests. They know that I'll keep them updated if there's anything that requires attention."

Brooke laughs. "Let me guess, the ladies bring you home-made cookies every time, don't they?"

"No." I stand up to put on another pot of coffee, then glance back over my shoulder, grinning. "Sometimes it's biscuits. Scones. If it's the right time of year, raspberry tarts."

She laughs, then glances out the window longingly. "You know, it's a beautiful day for sketching. Soft light, just warm enough for a leisurely stroll..."

"I should be done by two or three today. We could drive down to Maple Trail and go for a bit of a walk. Or drive up to one of the lookouts."

"Or..." Her fingers trace circles on the wooden table. "I could take my car and follow you to the clinic. I could meet your special lady friends"...she raises an eyebrow and giggles..."and we could have our sandwiches. Then I could go for a short drive and do some sketching until two thir-tyish and meet you back at the clinic?"

Every fiber of my being screams *No*. I want her with me. Or I want to know exactly where she is. There are some dangerous areas up here on the mountain, and Brooke isn't from here. My head begins to spin with all the ways someone who doesn't know their way around the area could get hurt.

But there's no way I can tell her that. She looks so hope-ful. If I begin deciding what she can and cannot do, that's not cool. I'm caught between the pull of needing her to be perfectly safe, and making sure I don't smother her.

"My beautiful artist needs some fresh air?" I force a smile. "Okay, no problem. When we're having lunch, I can go through a map with you and help you find anything specific you're looking for. Sounds good?"

It feels like I've said the right thing, and her warm smile floods me with relief.

"Sounds great. Now, do you normally wear a tuxedo for your visit with these important ladies, or..." I reach out to tweak her nose, sending us both into fits of laughter.

Brooke is already the most important lady in my life. Mrs. Jackson and her mother never stood a chance.

12

BROOKE

I was so sure that Jonah was the most incredible thing up here on Wolfe Mountain. Then I discovered the joy of genuine grandma-made vanilla raspberry tarts with cinnamon nutmeg pastry.

I'm kidding. He's still in the lead by miles. However, my world view of desserts has been turned on its head.

We finish up our sandwiches and eat another tart each, both of us practically moaning in bliss.

"I know people say not to compare food to sex," Jonah says with a grin and a few crumbs on his lip, "But *daaamn*."

"I was thinking the same thing! We're both terrible."

"Correction. Terrible *and* filled with raspberry goodness."

"Definitely the best kind of terrible." I stand up and clear away the containers and napkins, enjoying the way Jonah bites his tongue and lets me. I'm moving around much more freely today, but am still being careful.

He pulls out his laptop and opens a map of the area, pointing out some of the scenic areas that are closest to Old Hemlock Valley. I know that he doesn't want me to go very far, but up here on the mountain, with all these winding roads, every town is at least half an hour away.

In particular, I notice a scenic abandoned village with a little chapel just this side of Pinesley. If I went there, then into the town proper to see the square and their church, I could have quite a bit of material.

Jonah is assuming that I'm going to go sketch there in person. But I could just as easily take a bunch of reference photos and get back here by the time he's finished, and then do the sketches anytime.

"Lots of options," I say brightly, making a few notes.

"Please fill up at Valley Gas before you leave town."

"Will do. And my phone's at one hundred percent, so that's fine too."

He still looks concerned, but it's hard to tell exactly *how* concerned. I guess that's the sort of thing that comes with time – which really makes it hit home that Jonah and I have known each other less than a week.

Part of me kind of loves that he's so overprotective, but at the same time I'm really going to have to figure out where he draws those lines and decide if they're ultimately too close for comfort.

Jonah fills up a coffee thermos for me, then tucks a water bottle into my bag and walks me to the car. "I know I'm being fussy," he says, hugging me carefully so as not to hurt my rib. "But you don't know the mountain. Things can get rough out there. I just want you to be prepared. Please don't hesitate to call with any questions. Okay?"

"Okay. But I'm good. I promise."

"Great. Have fun." He gives me a kiss that I feel all the way down my thighs. Perhaps he's hinting what could be in store for me again tonight.

I have to admit, this electric physical connection

between us definitely makes me feel closer to him. I still don't want to rush anything. Although, when I think about it, I don't know what the natural course for these sorts of things is supposed to be...but I would assume it takes time to find a balance.

It's confusing.

Jonah must have called ahead, because when I get to the gas station, there's a big bruiser of a guy standing out front to welcome me. "Hey there, Brooke. I'll fill it up with premium, and make sure your windshield is nice and clean."

His jacket where it's stretched across his huge chest announces his name as Carson. Geez – are all the men around here jacked like bodybuilders?

Then he won't let me pay, insisting that it's already been taken care of.

As I drive off, my foot is a little heavier than it should be on the gas. *Grr.* Once again, is that caring or controlling? I mean, making sure I have enough gas for a drive is a sweet gesture. It's a nice thing that a husband would do for a wife. But... We're not there yet. Not even close. So... Is it too much? Is he overdoing it a little? I can't decide.

The winding drive around the mountain is delightfully tranquil — trees and rugged chunks of rocks, the odd squirrel racing across the road. The abandoned chapel outside of Pinesley is crumbling terribly, which makes for some amazing reference shots. The stone texture is incredible, as rough-hewn and rugged as the mountain itself.

I get to Pinesley around one-thirty, which only gives me about thirty minutes to take photos. I decide to text Jonah when I'm only fifteen minutes away from his clinic.

I park just outside of the town square at a public lot across from the church. The square itself is cobblestone, but the dirt or sand is missing from between the rocks, and nobody has done any landscaping in quite a while. Some of the flowerbeds are still interesting, though, with chipped antique planters.

I take a whole bunch of photos, losing all track of time. There's a path that leads to a laneway, with a perfectly curved split cedar fence that I can use in some future illustration. Since I don't know the trail, I don't go very far, but I do stop to take photos of a family of chipmunks before turning back.

Then I look around at this street more carefully. The entire town seems to be kind of...falling down. As if nobody's bothering to look after it.

Walking slowly, I take photos of interesting details until I'm at the chipped sidewalk in front of the old church I read about.

It's not aging beautifully. It looks like...a crack-house. One of the stained glass windows at the side has been boarded up, with graffiti sprayed all over the plywood. Smashed beer bottles lie strewn around the entrance. The large stone urns that once held flowers have long since been kicked over, one of them shattered right through the center.

One of the front windows is wedged half-open with a board, and the rotting front door is slightly ajar, hanging askew on its hinges.

My thumb keeps tapping my phone, taking more photos. Even if this place is a decrepit dump, I might be able to use the references at some point. I can always tidy things up as little when I sketch it.

I look down to check the last few photos to make sure they're bright enough. When my chin lifts, I'm staring directly at two guys in filthy jeans and faded, baggy t-shirts. They're unnaturally thin, with hollow eyes that definitely suggest an overuse of a variety of illicit substances.

"Hipster wannabe influencers ain't welcome around here," the taller one in a gray t-shirt chuckles, coming closer.

"Dunno. Maybe she thinks we're movie stars." The guy with the scraggly beard comes closer, his gait uneven.

Backing away slowly, I try a slight smile. "It's an interesting old church." Something that I read once echoes in the back of my mind...that the more you humanize yourself to an attacker, the less inclined they might be to hurt you. I'm not sure what these guys are after, but it's worth a shot. "My grandma loves old churches, so I collect photos of them for her," I lie smoothly.

It's hard to tell how old these guys might be. Late twenties? Early forties? They both have deep tans from being outdoors a lot, but there's no warmth to their skin tone. Almost as if it wants to be gray.

"Aww, a good little grandma's girl," Scraggly Beard drawls, his shirt hitching up as he scratches his belly. "That's sweet."

"She's from out of town – I haven't seen that car before, have you?" Gray Shirt points across the square to where my crappy old station wagon is parked.

They keep approaching me slowly with a nonchalance that is almost sinister.

Glancing around, I realize I probably look like a frightened rabbit. There's nobody else out here on the streets, even though it's the middle of the day. Even though they don't look very strong, there's still two of them, and no way could I fight them off. Plus, there's an entire uneven cobblestone square between me and my car.

My knees knock as I take another step backward.

Right now, this frightened little rabbit wishes that she had her Wolfe.

13

JONAH

A dark prickling sensation starts up between my shoulder blades as soon as Brooke drives away.

I really shouldn't be this worried. She managed to survive in the world just fine long before she met me. All she's doing is driving around a bit and sketching a little. I assume she'll take some photos along the way, too.

So why do I still feel like I shouldn't have let her go alone?

I *wanted* to tell her not to go without me. Insisted that I drive her myself in just a couple of hours. But there was something in her eyes telling me that she needed her space, which I understood completely. I was a loner myself my entire life until I met Brooke.

Dammit. I wish that she could have her personal space without driving all over the mountain alone.

Luckily, my afternoon appointments are simple, and I finish early since Mr. Emmerdale called to cancel, explaining that his wife talked him into going to see his regular doctor tomorrow to get some tests...which is probably for the best, to be honest.

Just as I pick up my phone to text Brooke, it rings in my hand. "Oh – hey, Clark."

"Jonah, look..." He sounds uncomfortable. "I don't mean to overstep any bounds or anything, but I feel like I should tell you something..."

"Go ahead."

"I had to do some errands today, and one of them was dropping off a few things at my cousin's mother-in-law's in Pinesley."

A bad feeling washes over me as I sink heavily into a chair.

"I was just leaving when I saw Brooke driving into town. It looked like she was heading straight to the town square, maybe."

"The church is right there, isn't it?"

"Yeah. You know it?"

"Yeah. She wanted to sketch churches today. When was this?"

"Maybe two minutes ago? Sorry, I gotta go. I'm in a huge rush today. But you know that right near the church is where all the—"

I'm already on my feet, grabbing my keys and racing for the truck. "I know. On my way. Thanks."

Nobody should ever speed on the mountain roads. It's dangerous. But I know these mountains like the back of my hand, and my truck has a surprising amount of power and handles corners well. After making it to Pinesley in record time, I head straight for the church.

Brooke's car is across the square in a mostly empty parking lot. I can't see anyone anywhere.

Shit.

My knuckles tighten on the steering wheel as my foot jams the brake all the way to the floor. I screech to a stop in front of the church. The whole place is filthy. There's no way she would have gone inside that dilapidated old building.

I jump out and begin running down the alley behind the church, hollering at the top of my lungs.

"Brooke!" I probably look like I'm out of my mind.

I am.

The blood in my veins turns to acid as I arrive in the tiny back parking lot. Two greasy little creeps are leading Brooke to one of several rickety benches where people are passing around a bottle.

She's mumbling, "No, really, I have to go..." but one of them has a hand clamped on her shoulder.

There are several more guys lounging around, along with a few too-thin, dull-eyed women. "Aww, come on. All girls like to party," the guy with the half-assed attempt at a beard says. "Come have a drink with us, Grandma's Girl."

I'm already charging toward them with a bellow. *"Get your fucking hands off her. Now."*

They release her so fast that Brooke stumbles a bit, wide-eyed and terrified.

The two guys already have their filthy hands in the air. "Hey, man," the guy in the ripped gray t-shirt says, "we were just inviting her to party." Yeah, right. From their glassy eyes, I know exactly what kind of party they mean.

My voice echoes off the nearby stone walls. "You heard her. She said no."

I want to tear them apart until I can hear their bones breaking, but I refuse to be violent in front of Brooke.

She steadies herself, then rushes into my arms. Holding her close, I stroke her hair. "It's okay, baby. I'll take you home."

She looks up at me with a timid smile, whispering, "Thank you." Then she looks around my arm and gasps.

A junker of a dirt bike has appeared out of nowhere, heading straight for us. There are two wild-eyed guys on it, one driving, the other with his arm outstretched as if he's after Brooke's purse. Wedged as we are between an old van and the stone wall of the church, there's nowhere for us to go.

I have exactly one second to decide what to do before they drive into us.

Grabbing Brooke tightly against me, I cradle the back of her head with one hand to hold it against my chest. Spinning so that my back is toward the creeps, the front end of their bike just misses me by a hair. I use the leverage of my foot against the wall to shove my hip into the side of the small vehicle, tipping it over.

Two rough yells fill the air, followed by a grinding noise as they flip hard and fast to the side, landing on the right legs of both riders and pinning them to the ground.

Still holding Brooke in my arms, I can feel her shaking. Part of me wants to destroy these horrible people for frightening her, but honestly it's more important that I get her out of here.

"It's okay," I murmur, carrying her as I jog back down the alley and to my truck. "We're going home."

There's no way I'm letting her drive herself right now, and I don't want to have to come back to this hellhole for her car. Luckily I have a trailer hitch that fits, so I tow her car to the edge of town before stopping and pulling over.

I turning toward her. "Are you really okay?"

"Yes, thank you." Her lovely eyes are huge. "I'm sorry. I didn't know. I just thought, you know...a small-town church. A few reference photos. What could possibly go wrong?"

I sigh heavily. "No, it's my fault. I didn't tell you the full story about this dump." Reaching out, I take her hands in mine. She yelps, her left hand twitching. My heart is instantly in my throat. "What is it?"

Her bottom lip quivers. "When you turned me away from that bike, I was so sure it was going to hit us. And I flung my arm out against the wall and...um... I hit my wrist on the bricks. I'm sorry. Like I said before, I've always been a bit clumsy."

Holding it gently, I straighten her wrist. "Show me where?" She points, and I run my thumb along the spot, stopping the second she flinches.

"I'll just be careful with it for a few days. I'm right-handed, so, you know. It's fine."

It isn't fine at all. I can detect serious pain.

I want to punch myself for allowing her to get hurt on my watch again. Not that I could have done much more in that split second, but still. If my sweet girl is hurt, I hurt.

"The hospital in West Stoneburg is twenty minutes from here. Can you be brave for me that long?"

"Of course."

I set her hand carefully on her knee. "Don't move that." Throwing the truck into gear, I head for the hospital, going as fast as I dare while towing a car.

Brooke's head rests back against the seat as she stares out at the trees, breathing slowly, trying to calm herself down.

My sweet girl is steadier than some soldiers would be in this situation. Maybe I'll make a mountain woman out of her yet.

14

BROOKE

Jonah calls the hospital to let them know we're on our way and will need an x-ray done, then reaches out to stroke my hair, flashing me a dazzling smile.

This is caring, not controlling. He knew there was a chance I wasn't safe on my own and he still didn't stop me.

And right now, he's more concerned about explaining the differences between a sprain, a fracture, and a break than saying, "I told you so."

I listen to his detailed descriptions, loving how enthusiastic he is when discussing the intricacies of the human body. I love the way he doesn't talk down to me, just shares his knowledge like he would with a colleague. Jonah is a genuinely smart guy, and I could listen to him forever.

Sure, my wrist *really* hurts if there's any kind of pressure on it. But it doesn't hurt nearly as much as the knowledge that I upset him by endangering myself. And yet... Our relationship has now officially taken its first hit of pressure, and Jonah's only thought is to care for me.

From the way he takes me into the hospital with his arm

around my shoulders, he might as well be waving a neon sign saying "My girl. Hands off." I think I like it.

I'm second in line for the x-ray machine, and after the technician does the imaging Jonah waits with me for the doctor to appear. All the while, he's distracting me with plans of what he's going to cook me for dinner, talking about all the nutrients that help bones heal.

"What if nothing is cracked, though?" I laugh. "Then can we just order in pizza?"

He holds my right hand gently and shakes his head. "Out here you can only order pizza for delivery on Friday and Saturday nights. Otherwise, you have to pick it up from town yourself. Or, if you're me, you keep the ingredients on hand to make it fresh."

A motherly woman in a white coat appears and brings us into a small room to go over the x-ray with us. Jonah joins Dr. Biro in discussing the hairline fracture. It's clear that they've worked together many times before.

Standing up, I peer at the light box closely. "Where's the fracture? I don't see anything."

"Right here." Dr. Biro points to a faint shadowy line. "It's slight, but it's there. Since you're a responsible adult and clearly have a medic with you, let's go with a brace. You can take it off to shower but make sure to keep it on otherwise. Just remember RICE: Rest, Ice, Compression, Elevation. Jonah knows the drill. Do not put any weight or pressure on it at all. The less you use it for the next three weeks, the better. If it feels like it's getting worse, come back and we'll do a cast. Okay?"

"Okay. Big question, though: is it a light enough crack that we can have pizza tonight, or should we start with the bone-fusing vegetables immediately?"

Dr. Biro laughs, then shoots Jonah a look. "I like her. She's a keeper."

"I know." He smiles proudly, making my heart actually expand in my chest. I wonder if that would show up on an x-ray?

As they talk about painkillers, and braces, and ice packs, I watch Jonah's deep eyes. His focus as he listens to the doctor and his attention to detail as evidenced by his questions is admirable.

Once my left hand and wrist are immobilized in a surprisingly comfortable blue brace, Jonah is extra careful helping me into the truck. Before he starts the engine, I say, "Hey, I need to explain something."

He turns and reaches over to hold my knee. "I'm listening."

A deep breath flows through me. I already know that he won't see me as broken or strange. He's the steadiest man I've ever met, and he always seems to want the facts. And yes, I can tell he is truly listening to me.

"My father controlled my mother completely. Every penny she spent, everywhere she went."

He nods. "I was starting to wonder if it was something like that. Go on."

"He wasted all her money. Racked up debt. Ruined her life, then took off when I was nine." I stare down at my hands, picking at the brace. "She eventually managed to make more money, get out of debt, fix her life. But the way he controlled her while he was still with us..." My head shakes. "It's like how someone who was attacked by a mountain lion is going to spend the rest of their life looking over their shoulder, you know what I mean?"

"Absolutely. It's only logical that you're going to be extra sensitive about that."

Looking into his deep green eyes, I melt. He didn't say *over*-sensitive, as in, I'm a helpless, hyper-emotional girl. He said *extra* sensitive. As if my childhood glitches are simply a part of me that needs a little longer to heal.

"Yeah. So, what I'm saying is, it might take some time to lower my shields, but I'd like to try. You know...if you would."

He turns his thick shoulders so he can rest his right hand along the back of my neck, his fingers sliding into my hair. His left hand squeezes my knee gently. Every gesture he makes is both comforting and sends a wild zing of excitement zipping through me.

"Brooke, I never want to control you. Ever. But I do have a deep, inexplicable urge to keep you safe."

He takes a deep breath, choosing his words carefully.

"It's not controlling. It's...caring. I'm never going to force you to do something or forbid you from doing something. I'll only ask you to take reasonable precautions. Like not hiking alone. And not visit a skeezy town like Pinesley alone. Is that fair?"

"Perfectly fair."

"If you want to dye your hair green, I'll drive you to the salon, and try not to make cracks about you blending into the forest. If you want to go skydiving, I'll be upset, but I'll help you find the place with the best safety record." He sighs heavily. "Okay, I *really* want to forbid you from skydiving, but that's the only thing. Anything else, we'll work it out together."

The way his smile lights up his eyes makes me melt. "I know you'll be safe here in Old Hemlock Valley. At least, you will be once you learn the roads a bit. Then you'll be free to go wherever you want, and I won't freak out." Thick fingers squeeze my knee. "We'll figure it out. Go over maps. Give us some time and we'll be a two-person team whose mission it is to keep you safe and happy. Sounds good?"

I nod enthusiastically, and we laugh together. It's the most comforting feeling in the world. "I think that's the most I've ever heard you say at once."

His eyes widen. "You know what, you're right. Other than about medical issues, you're the only person I've ever really felt comfortable talking to."

"I like that. But it sounds as if you have plenty of friends? Carson at the gas station. And you sent Clark to check on me, for goodness' sake."

"Yeah, but we only talk about practical things. Weather, roads, trucks."

"I already talked to Ernest about tractors, I can learn how to talk about trucks too." I laugh. "Oh, and thanks for the gas. I think the premium might have been wasted on my poor ol' beater, but Carson got my windshield cleaner than it's ever been." My right hand covers his on my knee. "I'm so sorry that I didn't listen to your warning. I'll be more careful in the future."

"Yes. And I can be a little more open. You might not have gone to Pinesley at all, if I'd told you more about it. So we'll have to work on you becoming a mountain woman, and me...well, becoming a relationship guy, I guess."

My mouth falls open with a dramatic gasp. "Wow, did you just say the forbidden word?"

The slight sun lines at the corners of his eyes crinkle as he grins. "*Re-la-tion-ship.* Yeah, I guess I did." Jonah straightens up and pulls out his phone. "Now, what do you want on your pizza? It'll be ready for pickup by the time we're driving through the valley."

15

JONAH

I'm delighted that Brooke truly loves Jim's Pizza, since it's the only pizza joint in town.

We get our order to go and enjoy dinner in my dining room, facing the window so we can enjoy the sunset. Thankfully, this time she finally takes a painkiller without making a face.

The pizza with spinach, sautéed onion, and spicy chicken, with a side of garlic breadsticks, are both incredible. We fall into a long drawn-out conversation speculating if pizzerias secretly read people according to their topping choices, like reading tea leaves.

"That would be incredible," Brooke laughs. "If there's ever an axe murderer in town, just ask Jim's employees. They'll know who it is, for sure. Just look for the guy who orders extra anchovies with barbecue sauce."

"I love your mind." Reaching out, I drag my thumb across her lower lip, pretending I'm wiping away sauce when really I just need to touch her. "You're always thinking of something new."

"Oh, my *mind*, huh?"

Gazing into her luminous gray eyes, I can almost hear the metallic click in the back of my brain as the realization snaps into place. Taking her right hand, I kiss the back of it. "I love all of you, Brooke."

Her lips fall open, and I swear she stops breathing for several seconds. Then she sputters, blinking. "I... I love you too. I just didn't think..."

"Because it's all happened so fast we haven't had time to think, baby." Shifting closer, I wrap my arm around her. "You were hurt, and I had to take care of you."

"Saved my life, you mean."

Shaking my head, I continue. "Then you had to heal, then this whole incident today—"

"Where you saved me again." Her palm strokes my cheek. "I think I'm always going to be safer with you around."

"In that case, it would probably be best if you move in right away. You know, safety first and all that."

Her voice is barely a whisper. "Really?"

"Yes. I'd suggest driving to your apartment and packing up immediately, but I don't want you stressing that wrist. So for now we can just plan everything, and then we can go in two or three weeks. Fair warning, I'll still do all the packing so that you don't lift anything."

Her lips press together as she tries to pull a mean face and fails. "*Grrr.*"

"Sweetie, come on. What kind of a medic would I be if I let you hurt yourself?"

Brooke's instant grin is pure sunshine. "I know you're just trying to keep me safe. So, yes. I'd love to move in with you. But I can pack up my own underwear drawer, thank you very much."

My eyes grow wide. "Are you saying you have a naughty things drawer that you don't want me to see?"

"I am not!"

"Yes, you are. I bet you don't want me to see your beef-cake magazines. Like *Lumberjack Quarterly*."

"Stop it." She smacks my shoulder lightly.

"*Shirtless Mountain Men Daily*."

"I'm serious, stop!"

"*Hard Wood*? I bet that's your favorite."

Leaning in, I cut off her giggle with a kiss. I had intended it to be sweet, but in three seconds her fingers are gripping the back of my hair tightly. "What are you trying to say, gorgeous?"

I swear there's a faint blush across her cheeks as she smiles. "Um, after all of today's excitement, I just wondered if...you know. Instead of dessert, maybe we could..."

"Say no more." I scoop her into my arms, kicking the chair out of the way as I carry her to the bedroom. Setting her on the bed, I slowly peel off her jeans, then her baggy t-shirt and tank top, leaving her in nothing but dark blue panties. I kind of love that she wears loose, casual clothing, so that nobody can see her luscious figure but me.

Brooke looks down, then laughs. "Oh my god, my underwear matches my brace. Is that the clumsy girl version of coordinating lingerie sets?"

"Don't worry, I'll be buying you all the lacy things you want next time we go to a bigger city." Looking down at her luscious figure, I growl. "Correction. All of the lacy things *I* want."

I lie her back on the bed, grabbing a small pillow to tuck against her left side. The bruising on her ribs isn't nearly as bad as I'd feared, thank goodness. But the pillow gives her something to slightly grip with her fingers to keep her wrist still.

Slowly pulling off my t-shirt, I realize I've never felt sexier than when Brooke is looking at me. There's something about her. She's the only person who's ever brought out this side of me and made me feel like a truly masculine being.

Like a wolf.

Lying over her, I keep my weight away from her body while a deep, powerful kiss consumes us both. She moans when I move away, kissing down her tender stomach to spread her legs.

I'm not nearly as gentle as I was last time. Diving in, I bathe her pussy with my tongue until her good hand is practically tearing out my hair.

Looking up, I love the way her expression tells me everything I need to know. That she likes it hard and fast. That she loves it when I slide my middle finger deep inside her, my palm facing up to press against her g-spot. That she adores the sensation of her swollen clit being massaged between my lips.

I don't know if it's love, or our connection, or maybe the way I've been trained to study people's feelings and read body language. Regardless, Brooke is incredibly responsive, her hips bucking up as if encouraging me.

"Mine," I growl, before dragging my tongue around and across her clit. The faster I move, the faster she pants.

Her juices are so sweet, and I hope that she can see in my eyes that I'm going to be between her legs every single day for the rest of our lives.

"Oh," Brooke moans, her chest heaving, her perky breasts bouncing up and down. "Yes... *Yes...*"

Her hot, wet pussy tenses around my fingers as she comes, her inner muscles rippling around me as I steadily lick her sensitive bud until she shakes from head to toe.

"Wow." Her voice is shaky. "That was...intense."

Licking softly, I wait until her climax subsides before jumping to my feet. Her eyes blaze as my jeans hit the floor.

I don't think I've ever been this thick and hard. Pre-come is already dripping from the tip of my cock as I settle over her. I devour her mouth as I drag the head of my cock through her wet slit, teasing her until she squirms, trying to pull me deeper.

"A month from now, after your wrist has healed completely, I want you on top of me. I want your hands on my chest as you lift your hips up and down, fucking yourself on my cock."

Brooke nods eagerly, then she grins. "I think I like it when the town medic talks dirty."

"It's all your fault." I dip inside her barely an inch, just enough to make her gasp. "You make me a savage animal, gorgeous."

"And you make me..." She looks up at me, smiling shyly. "Feel complete. Is that stupid cheesy?"

"As cheesy as Jim's pizza. But that's not a bad thing. It's also the truth."

Sinking deeply into her tight pussy feels like the most natural thing in the world. I listen carefully to her breath, wanting to know exactly how much pressure she needs. After a few incredibly slow strokes, she nods, gripping the back of my neck, and I feel her legs wrap around me.

I pull out, bumping over her clit, watching her quiver before plunging in again. As I stare down at the incredible sight of my cock sliding in and out of her delicate pink folds, a sense of perfect completeness washes over me.

I don't believe in fate. I don't even know if I believe in soulmates. But I do know I sure as the sun rises in the East and sets in the West that Brooke and I will be together forever.

We were meant to be.

16

BROOKE

I'm shaking, melting, quivering. Every single spot where Jonah touches me turns to liquid fire.

It's so intense. It feels *too* good. Like when a hot tub is just a little too hot, but you still feel your muscles unclenching.

Jonah's pace increases, his thick, brutally hard cock thrusting inside me faster and deeper. There's no need to be afraid anymore, even when things are intense. I know that he's the one. That we're together for good.

Gripping the back of his short hair, I pull his head up from where he's nibbling on my nipple as he glides deep inside me.

"I love you," I whisper as I stare deeply into his eyes. "I just wanted to say it first this time."

He grins, the faint crinkles around his eyes deepening. "I love you so much, baby." His pace slows and he pulls almost all the way out, then eases inside so gradually that I gasp.

"And as soon as your wrist heals, we're gonna start physiotherapy to build up the strength in your left hand."

"So I can hold on for dear life when I'm riding you in bed?"

"That, plus you're going to be lifting a very large diamond on that hand every day for the rest of your life."

It was clear from the second we met that Jonah is a very serious person. I know he's not teasing. My hand slides down and underneath his arm to grip the back of his shoulder. "You know, you're very handsome for a crazy dude with no impulse control."

Now it's his turn to growl before rubbing his nose against mine. "Baby, you have no idea how much I'm holding back."

A deep tremble runs through me. He's not kidding about this, either. As soon as my injuries have healed, I can just imagine how wild my mountain man is going to be.

I already know that he's going to take me in every room of the house, and in his truck, and on the forest trails. I'm going to become one of those women who always keeps an extra pair of panties in her purse, just in case.

Jonah thrusts harder, shattering my already fragmented train of thought. I didn't think his huge cock could get any thicker, but it feels like it does as his breath becomes slightly choppy. His hand slides to my breasts, then tugs gently at my nipples while I moan. Sparks of pleasure zing through me as I feel the pressure building fast.

The sensations are so intense. Are they really supposed to be so big? I can't believe that this kind of instant bonding is quite natural.

Just when I'm wishing I had a bit more pressure, Jonah's hand slides down between us, his thumb flicking across my clit.

"Fuck, how do you always know what I need?" I gasp.

"Because I was born to take care of you."

My laugh is cut off when he melds his mouth to mine. There are no more words, just pure raw sensation. His driving thrusts become rougher as he presses against my clit, rocking my body with his hips. Our kiss becomes frantic, uneven, both of us gasping yet not wanting to pull away.

An odd pang of pride blossoms through my chest as I feel Jonah losing control. *I did that.* This stoic, surly mountain man wants and needs me so much that he actually loses himself. It's strange, but it fills me with confidence.

My heels dig into the bed, hips thrusting up to meet him stroke for stroke, encouraging him on.

"Yeah," he grunts, gripping me hard. Three more savage strokes then we both cry out – mine a soft fluttery cry, and his a gritty growl. "*Mine.* My precious baby."

My pussy clenches hard around his shaft, squeezing him, milking him, as I feel his hot come shoot inside me. The climax tumbles over me like an ocean wave, leaving me almost dizzy as I sprawl under him.

Jonah rolls carefully to the side, as I snuggle against him. "That..." He shakes his head. "I mean, *damn*, girl."

"So eloquent. I was thinking the same thing."

My hand drifts down his chest to trace along his glistening abs. "After a workout like that, it's a shame we can't order more pizza for delivery."

"We just had—"

My finger drops to his lips. "Didn't you say that the calcium in cheese was excellent for healing hairline fractures?"

His voice is muffled as he mutters, "I said nothing of the sort."

"*So* weird. Because that's what I heard."

His teeth nip at my finger, then he pulls me closer,

stroking my hair. "If it will make my sweet girl happy, I'll put in a pizza oven."

"Really?"

"Yes, as long as I can get you a pizza paddle with an *extremely* long handle, and you promise not to burn yourself."

"I'm not that accident prone, you know."

He grins. "Could have fooled me. And you fell for me. There's clearly something wrong with you."

"It's all the river's fault for making me fall in the first place."

Jonah stares up at the ceiling. "And now I have to go thank the river. What a world."

"Yes, but it's our world," I laugh.

"Damn straight, baby. Ours. Forever."

EPILOGUE
JONAH

Staring at my lovely wife through the large library window, I think I could watch her sketch all day.

Brooke has always been the most breathtaking woman I've ever seen. It's like there's a light that surrounds her. As if all the love and sweetness in her heart radiates outward.

But now, after living with me for two years up on the mountain, she glows even more. It's not just all the fresh air and sunshine, or the faint tan that brought out a few more charming freckles. She's truly blossomed.

About a month after she settled into my – sorry – *our* house, she began working like crazy. When I gently suggested she scale back so that she didn't burn herself out, she simply raised a skeptical eyebrow.

Then Brooke spoke with Mrs. Honeywell at the library and started a drawing group in the large conference room every Tuesday afternoon while I'm busy at the clinic. She even called it "Drawing and Doodling for People Who Aren't Very Good at It" to ensure that everyone knew it was purely for fun and no pressure.

Now she has just as many friends around here as I do and keeps track of our social calendar. Apparently married couples are supposed to go out at least once a week until they have kids. I told her she must have snuck this into the fine print of our marriage license, but she wouldn't relent. She just made that little adorable *grr* sound that turns me on so much.

I watch in admiration as her quick hands move across the easel, her engagement and wedding rings sparkling in the sunlight. My thrifty girl designed our wedding invitations herself, using pressed flowers from the forest and her own sketches. We only invited a dozen people, but since it took place at City Hall, half the town showed up anyway.

She was just as beautiful in her simple white dress as she is now in a slouchy green sweater and yoga pants, leaning forward to point to something on another artist's drawing. Everyone in town tells me how kind Brooke is. And apparently, behind my back, they mention how much she's mellowed me out.

Tearing my gaze away from the window, I lean on my truck and idly check my email for ten minutes until Brooke comes out waving goodbye to people. I take her bag, then begin to help her into the truck, but stop.

Caging her against the seat with my arms, I lean down to nuzzle her throat. "You're very sexy when you're sketching. Did you know that?"

"Interesting. I had no idea." Her soft gray eyes lock on mine. "You're very sexy when you stare at me through the window like an overprotective husband."

"Ah, you noticed that?"

"Every. Single. Time." Her left hand reaches down and punctuates each word with a squeeze of my ass, and I can't help but notice that her grip strength is completely back to normal.

Since we can't keep our hands off each other, the wrist is something I've been paying attention to for a while. Sure, we attempt to be professional in the clinic, and when in public. But it's difficult.

Partly because my gorgeous little artist knows she can make me hard with no more than a sultry glance and a toss of her auburn hair. We're always jumping into bed for another round.

"You know, if we pick up pizza now, we'll finish dinner faster. Early bedtime." My eyebrows fly up and down suggestively.

Brooke fists the front of my t-shirt, pulling my mouth to hers for a deep, sensual kiss. The flash of heat is instant, as our bodies press together, each point of contact becoming warmer as we hold each other close. Then she pushes me away to laugh. "Or we could throw something in the oven that takes an hour to cook. If only we had something to do while we wait..."

I take hold of her hot, round ass with both hands. "How about that frozen casserole?"

"Perfect. Let's go."

～

Stay tuned for plenty of hot, burly (sometimes surly) men on Wolfe Mountain!
You'll see Jonah's brother Jace in **Found by the Surly Ranger**.

You'll see Carson again in the ***Dirty Brothers series*** starting September 2024.
You'll see Clark again soon in ***Protected by the Surly Carpenter***.

It couldn't have been eight minutes since Barrett made the call when a blue tow truck with "Valley Automotive" painted in friendly white letters on the side comes barreling into the lot.

Another lumberjack-sized man jumps out, but fortunately this one doesn't seem nearly as grouchy. He's smiling widely as he approaches. His gaze drifts over each of us, not in a leering way, but still reminding me that we're "the new girls in town". We've gotten a few curious glances already when we were downtown.

When his eyes lock on mine, his expression changes completely. The focus of his friendly smile shifts to his eyes as he approaches. He holds out his hand, shaking mine gently. "Hi. I'm Griffin."

There's something about the warmth of his palm against mine. Something in the look in his eyes and his incredible woodsy fragrance that feels even more grounding than the forest. I've never felt drawn to a man before, but right now my knees are literally quivering. He's gorgeous. Stunning.

Striking. I study linguistics and communications, yet I'm at a loss for accurate words beyond *holy crap*.

Finally, I manage to whisper, "Harper."

Barrett clears his throat. "They're staying at Riggs' place. I'll run these two there now. You good?"

"Sure." Griffin releases my hand but doesn't step away for a few more seconds. It feels like time itself is shifting, and every moment our gazes are locked on each other there's some kind of energy passing between us. My entire body is reacting to his presence: my breathing is getting faster. Heat is blooming through my core.

If just one look at this guy produces this much lust, how am I supposed to sit in a truck right beside him?

Finally I break the spell, tearing my gaze away and noticing Jocelyn and Nikki barely able to stifle their giggles as they walk with Barrett toward his truck.

Part of this summer was supposed to be about getting out of my comfort zone and trying new things. I was thinking that would mean hiking, living in a different town, and focusing on work that wasn't directly supervised. Not running into a guy who is so stunning that my ankles are legit stiff from trying to hold myself still. I struggle to keep myself from rocking side to side nervously as I watch him walk, his powerful body moving with such a relaxed gait that I'm kind of envious.

Griffin tries to start my car, getting that sad clicking sound again. He nods. "Yup, she's dead all right." He puts it in neutral and hooks it up to his truck with practiced movements, as if he's been doing this a very long time.

He looks to be around thirty and carries himself with a casual grace that's wildly sexy. That's it! He's wild. Like a panther. Six foot three or so, with thick, sculpted arms and a chest that can barely be contained by his thin charcoal t-shirt. And there's a cocky twinkle in his eyes when he flashes me a grin that isn't just handsome, it's charming as heck.

"All ready." He walks me over to the passenger seat of the tow truck, and my eyes land on the "Valley Automotive" lettering again.

I remember something that I can't help but blurt out. "Yesterday at the diner, someone said something about the tow truck service being run by dirty boys."

He's already pulling out his wallet to show me his driver's license. My throat makes an involuntary snort-laugh as I read his name. *Griffin Dirty.*

"Yup." His dark chuckle dances straight up my spine. "Our last name mostly died out across much of the country in the early nineteen hundreds, for obvious reasons. But here on the mountain, the Dirty family has kept the name alive."

"I didn't mean–"

"It's okay to laugh." His eyes twinkle and he leans in to whisper, "It's weird. I know."

His strong, rough hand takes mine to help me up into the truck and for half a second we're face to face, barely two inches apart, so close that I'm sure he can hear my heart hammering in my chest.

I've never felt this way around any man before. Lust, intrigue, and some sort of connection that feels like it was always there. Yet I haven't known him for even five minutes.

Is it possible that I'm falling for a Dirty boy?

∼

Griffin, Carson, and Walker Dirty – Three sexy mountain

man mechanics who have been hoping to find the right woman someday.

"Someday" happens in early September, 2024
Don't miss ***Dirty Whispers, Dirty Rumors, and Dirty Secrets.***

ALSO BY HALEY TRAVIS

Book links at haleytravisromance.com

Rescued by the Surly Woodsman

Be careful out in the woods. You might run into the love of your life.

This handsome older man doesn't seem to realize he's so sexy I can hardly breathe. He's as massive as the mountain, and nearly as quiet. He's extremely protective. Almost too much. This wild lust overtakes us both, but it seems too quick... Could this gorgeous mountain man truly be obsessed already?

Thin Ice - Winter Heat at Wolfe Mountain Chalet

He's a total stranger. Until I slip and fall into his arms, and then into his bed.

He claims he's a loner, but that doesn't explain why he's obsessed with me. Yet from the second he growls, "You're mine," into my ear, I want it to be true.

The Lumberjack's Quirky Girl

I probably shouldn't have ogled Braden Oakley's big axe. *Oops.*

Tall as a redwood and built like a moose, the devastatingly gorgeous lumberjack should have nothing in common with little miss artsy-pants—aka, *me*. So how come the harder I try to stay away, the more I end up wrapped up in his muscled arms begging for more of his hard...wood?

Possessing My Lily

From the second her delicate body thumped into my chest, I knew Lily was mine.

Every detail of my gorgeous, sweet girl is precious. I'll find a way to prove I'm worth getting through her fears. That my possession will be the best thing for both of us.

Her New Bodyguard: Jackson

It was supposed to be a simple personal security job. But Ashley was so sexy and innocent that my need to care for her was far more than professional.

Fake Summer Wife

I'd always been too timid. But when a gorgeous man needed a favor and asked me out in front of the whole diner, I had to say yes... I would be his phony wife for one night.

For new release updates from Amazon, go to the author's page, then click **+Follow** near the top left.

Please join the mailing list at haleytravisromance.com for new releases, updates, discounts & freebies!

www.ingramcontent.com/pod-product-compliance
Lightning Source LLC
Chambersburg PA
CBHW020452160726
47991CB00007B/2615